Land ^{of} _{the} Crystal Stars:

The Second Rise of Guardians

RIA MATHEWS

authorHOUSE®

AuthorHouse™
1663 Liberty Drive
Bloomington, IN 47403
www.authorhouse.com
Phone: 833-262-8899

Published by AuthorHouse 04/20/2022

ISBN: 978-1-6655-5787-0 (sc)
ISBN: 978-1-6655-5786-3 (e)

Print information available on the last page.

This book is printed on acid-free paper.

In loving memory of family and friends who have passed in the past year. To all the fans who have read about the characters and loves the story keep on reading.

The Crystal Star
of the Fire Realm

Prologue

"This is the Crystal Star of the Fire Realm has a breathtaking view; it is quite beautiful. It looks like fire living when the flowers blow in the wind. There are tulips, red roses, red daisies, and gardenias. They two had stepped out of the portal into a field of flowers. I think that we should stay here for the night until the fighting slows or comes to a stop." Sue suggested.

"I agree with you. It is one hell of a view. I never imaged that the Fire Realm was so beautiful in its own way. Then we can begin our search for the first of the 8 guardians in the morning. Let us go ahead and set up the tent from the rack sack that we brought with us. We can set up the camp before setting off first thing in the morning." Joey said.

As the two friends set up camp and are hoping that they will be able to find the Guardian of the Crystal Star of the Fire Realm. They are hoping more than anything to be able to show this scene to their friends. They know that the plan is to find each guardian and send them back to the Crystal Star of Water and Ice with messages for their friends. To let them to know things are okay with them and the search will continue for the rest of the Guardians', and the Star Princess too. The two friends worked on the camp, so they walked out of the tent to look for firewood. This way they can make a fire so they can make food. The fire will also provide heat and light when it gets dark. They two guardians set out to do their own tasks. Sue was responsibility for cooking and maintaining the fire for a little while. Joey's is responsibility for finding food, water, and more firewood for the fire, he is also on first watch. They did this until it started to get dark, and they are only a few miles away from the town. They ate grilled fish and some herbs they found along a small river they came across while exploring the area of their camp. This also provided them with water. They had the equipment for cooking just needed to find the other stuff. They put water in their thermos to take with them in the morning when they start looking for the next guardian. They heard fighting in the distance and was getting nervous about the fighting getting to close to their camp.

The fighting continue late into the night till early morning and Sue is on watch it is around 1:30a.m. She started to worry that the fighting would fall into their camp dragging them into the fighting that has nothing to do with them. She decided to wake Joey up even though he had already done his shift. More so because the fighting seemed to get closer to them which made her even more nervous.

"Joey wakes up; there seems to be trouble. I can see fire in the town that isn't far from us." Sue said shaking Joey awake.

"I'm up. What has you worried?" Joey asked her.

"The fighting seems to be getting closer to our camp. Why have we not been attacked?" Sue asked out loud and is wondering with a frown.

"There is always claim before the storm. Let us keep our guard up because you never know when an attack will come. If you haven't noticed the fighting has claimed down as well." Joey replied.

"Okay I will pay more attention. Are you going to release your summons?" Sue said.

"No, I'm going to keep my dragon here for the time being she can help us keep watch for the rest of the night." Joey said.

Chapter 1

➤⊶⟡⊷⟐⊶⟡⊷⟢⊷◄

𝒯he two friends woke at 3:30a.m. in the next morning because of the fighting was starting to get to close to their camp. They started to pack up the camp before the fighting gets any closer. They set out before dawn and started looking for the Guardian of the Crystal Star of the Fire Realm. The thing is that they did not know if the guardian was going to be a guy or a girl. This is going to take a little while to find some information that they might need about the Crystal Star of Fire Realm. They fly down the mountain to start their search for the next guardian. As the two friends look around to see where to start, they notice off in the distance a small town for which they did notice the night before but couldn't see if it is a banded or has people living there. With the fighting from last night, its good chance that the town's people might not be accepted to strangers walking into their town.

"Is there any coffee that we can drink being so earlier in the morning. Then start are search over there, Sue points in the direction of east. Should we start looking in that small town over there, it looks like maybe a day or two walk from our camp site in the field? It looks like we may have to camp outside again today and tonight." Sue asked.

"Dear cousin does believe that we did bring some forgers coffee with us and a camping coffee pot, along with camping bowls, plates, cups, utilizes, pans, and you might be onto something. I think we should at least try there because we do need more information. Jenny said that "Each guardian girl or guy; are prince or princess of their own realm, maybe we might find out who the person is to become the guardian of this realm. Let us look at the town it may take a day or two from our estimate, but if I use one of my summon, we could get there in a day or less." Joey replied.

"Even if that sounds like a good plan, we could use it for a little bit but don't use to much of your powers we might need them later. We also don't want to scare the town's people by just showing up on a dragon out of nowhere." Sue said.

Joey released his summons of the light dragon so that he could maintain his energy and powers. Sue had released her powers the night before so that she would not feel drained of her powers and energy. The two of them started to walk towards the town. Sue was wondering what they would find there and who they would find there whether they be friend or foe. They knew that this would not be easy because of very little information they were given from the mystery guy the other night during the dance.

The two kept walking and would only stop to rest and eat they knew that it was going to take a little while before they reach the small town. They wanted to take their time, so they don't get rushed or a surprise attack by an enemy. As they keep walking. It started to get dark, and the sky looked as if it were bleeding in the distance. That the realm seemed to be at peace, which was never a good thing when it comes to being in a strange place. As they kept walking, they choose to set up camp again and this time it was in a field of flowers that were so colorful that it looked as if the flowers were showing a rainbow. They stood there looking at the scene before them. They got out their camping stuff, set up the tent in a bare spot that isn't covered with flowers.

"This should be a good spot for tonight." Joey said.

"Yeah, I agree. We need to rest because; we should be in the town by late noon. What should we eat tonight?" Sue said.

"I agree with you. What we can eat will have to be nuts and some other vegetables that we still have left from last night. There is a little bit of fish that was cooked already and still good." Joey said.

"If that is all we, have I can deal with it. At least it will be something to put into our stomach that way we have some type of energy. We are going to need it as we take turns to keep watch." Sue said back.

I will take the first watch, and you can get some rest, and then release me in 3 hours." Joey said.

"Okay, I will rest; wake me when it is time for my turn for watch, and then we need to head out at first break of dawn, okay." Sue said.

"Agreed. Let us get some rest because that also will give us some energy to help fight off an enemy if we get attack in the middle of the night. Let us get to sleep early that way we can set off at dawn like you suggested." Joey said. Sue went inside the tent to set up the sleeping bags and pillows for Joey and herself. She stepped back outside to sit down beside Joey and look at the view which is just as beautiful as the first view they saw stepping out of the light portal. She then went back into the tent an hour later to get in bed to rest after a long walk from the mountain top to the town. She didn't realize that the town was so far. Right now. she needed to rest, because if there is an attack in the middle of the night Joey would be the only one who could defend them from enemies. Sue defeated off to sleep, which was an uneasy sleep, she kept dreaming of the Dark Prince, Dark Queen, Dark King, and the Dark Kingdom Zodiac, every night since the fight to free Alena. She would wake from a deep sleep, in sweat; wondering why she could not shake the feeling that something was going to happen to both Alena and Leroy when Joey and her, are not there.

The dream is always about the darkness which seems to follow the Dark Kingdom Zodiac. It is as if her light was going dimed and all can she see if darkness, where there should be light there isn't any.

She felt that the darkness would sallow her up and all the light and become the darkness at any time. Then she would see this bright white light and someone in it. She reaches for this bright white light so she can try and feel the warmth that is radiating off it. It felt of love, faith, happiness, and everything good and great. Whoever was letting it off this light seemed so peaceful, when she would get chose to see who was in the light that would be when she wakes from the dream.

>-+-+>-•-<+-+-<

Joey was sitting at the entrance to the tent they share. Which they carried in a ruck shack. They had pack food and water for the trip so that they have prerevision while they travel from one realm to another. They would ride on the light dragon which is on one of Joey's dragons. As he had to summon the Light Dragon to carry them and their stuff. Which it also must carry Sue and him, that way they are free to defend themselves from an enemy attack if it so happens to come down to that.

Joey is sitting there; he starts to see the land in front of him and he is drawn to it as if he was a part of it. Sue was right the land was very beautiful and it did seem to be at peace at night at least. During the day it might be a little ruff with all the fighting. Something had hit him in a flash bang like a flash grenade. Then something happened and Joey had passed out, he could not even yell for Sue to give a warning to get away from whatever was coming for them. His body was already hitting the ground, then he passed out and the darkness took him. Sue was passed out asleep in the tent, but she was going to stay that way for a while.

⊱ ⊹ ⟡ ⊙ ⟡ ⊹ ⊰

Joey and Sue are taken to another camp that is a way from the town they were going to start their searching for the guardian of the Fire Realm.

Joey could smell a mixture of spices and the ones he can make out are cloves, orange, apple cinnamon, and a strong but not too overwhelming of sage. This mixture didn't seem to be harmful to them. It seems to be waking him up and when his eyes started to adjust to the deem light, he could make out a hut that had red covers on one wall, tribal patterns on another wall, and a door that had a cover over it in the color red. Joey started to really wake and make out his surroundings. It is easy to tell that there are people around and they are heavily armed. His first thought was to get Sue and get the hell out of there as fast as they can. The mixture of spices was also starting to make his power somewhat weak which is never good in a hostel situation.

What has Sue and him walk into? This was not going to be easy or even a chance of escape from these people. Joey looked over to see that Sue was there and is still passed out. He tried to sit up to have a better view of the hut that they are in, but someone hit him in the temple which caused him to see spots in is eyes and he started to get pissed off.

"The next person to hit me or my cousin is going to wish they was some where else or dead. Cause that is what they are going to face when I lose complete control." Joey warned. That was when Sue started to stir. She opened her eyes to see where she is and she squinch her nose up to the smell of the mixed spices.

Sue was asleep in the bed, and the next thing she knew she had woken from a dead sleep. There were people all around, staring at her and she could not move as if she was being held down by something.

"What is going on here?" Sue demanded.

"Well, I see she is finally awake." Odd person said from the back.

"Who are you? Where am I? Where is Joey?" Sue asked.

"You are in Everest Town. The handsome guy, you ask about; is very good looking, is he your boyfriend?" Odd person said.

"First of all, Joey is his name, and he is my cousin. Second is this the town that was on that dirt road?" Sue said.

"Does he have a girlfriend? Yes, this is that town you were heading too yesterday." Odd person said.

"Yes, what is your name? What time is it?" Sue asked.

"It is Lola, and the time is 1am." Lola said.

"It is nice to meet you, Lola. Thanks for giving me the time, were Joey at?" Sue asked.

"He is sleeping in the next room. I wanted to talk to you first. Why are you here in my realm? What are you?" Lola asked.

"First of all, my name is Sue Stang, I'm 15 years old, born June 15, I am a second former in high school. I am also the guardian of Light and Travel. My crystal star is The Crystal Star of Light and Travel." Sue answered.

"Leave her alone!!" Joey said.

As everyone turned around, they saw that he had come too and walked out of the room. He did not understand what was going on or why they were questioning Sue. All he knew was they needed to find the guardian of the Crystal Star of Fire, and these people were wasting their time. Sue had looked up and saw that Joey was somewhat hurt, and it had to be from these people who ever they are.

"I see you are awake." Lola said with a smile.

"I told you to leave her alone." Joey said with angry.

"All we want to know is why you two are here?" Lola said.

"Then I will tell you." Joey said.

"Fine, then explain." Lola said.

"My name is Joseph Ryan, I'm a guardian of summon, my Crystal Star is the Summoning Star. We are looking for the 8 guardians of the Majestic Star Kingdom, so that we can find the star princess. We are looking for one of the eight guardians here in this realm with the gift of fire power and are the Guardian of The Crystal Star of Fire." Joey said.

"So, I see you are looking for someone who has this special gift. Well guess what you have found her. I am the guardian you seek." Lola said.

"Are you for real?" Sue and Joey said together.

"Yeah, why is it so hard to believe?" Lola asked.

"We were told that the guardians are prince or princess of their realm." Sue said.

"Well, there are some changes that need to be made then. You see at one time my family ruled this realm with loving care until we were taken over by people from another dark place and which my parents were killed, and they had adopted me out to a family who did not have much but could love me for who I am." Lola said.

There has been fighting in the realm of fire for so long that the royal family had been forgotten which made it safe for Lola to grow up and become who she is now. As time went on, she could not understand why she was different from everyone else. So, she kept her powers a secret from her adopted parents and went on living as if there was no change. The day came when the dark people would come back, and her powers started to awaken in the past few years.

"So don't be shocked. Yes, these dark people came just recently and started to change each tribe and turn them against each other when we have had peace for years until a few months ago." Lola said.

"I see; you came into your powers just recently." Joey said.

"Yes, that is true." Lola said.

"Then we need your help. If we can find the other 8 guardians, we can put a stop to their power taking over everything." Sue said.

"First you must help me. If you want me to come with you and find the other guardians as you say, first we need to get to the castle so we can get the most important thing to this realm. If you say you are from the Majestic Star Kingdom, then there is something at the castle you will need." Lola said.

"Then we will help you and your people to be at peace again." Sue said.

"I agree with you." Joey said.

Chapter 2

>─┼─◇─◦─◯─◦─◇─┼─<

"Then it is settled we will leave at first dawn." Lola said.

Lola is a long red hair girl, with fair skin, she has light blue eyes, she stands about 5'6", and her age is 16 years old. She was born into the royal family of The Crystal Star of Fire but was adopted by a loving couple who could not have children, when the royal family had been overthrown by the Dark Kingdom Zodiac. Lola's true parents were forced to give her up so that she had a chance at a normal life, but life for Lola was not normal she had powers that could be control by her which is fire and ice fire, and she can make the fire do what she wanted. It was hard for her growing up because the people fared her powers, and the children would tease her about it.

>─┼─◇─◦─◯─◦─◇─┼─<

Meanwhile on the Crystal Star of Water and Ice Jennifer, Glen, Leroy, and Alena are watching their friends go into the light portal that is connected to space while they ride on the back of the light dragon for which Joey had summoned. They were thinking is if their friends had made it okay to the Fire Realm.

"I hope they will be fine without us there to help them." Alena said.

"Have faith and believe in your friends, that they made it okay. Also have faith that they will be okay and complete their mission without a hitch. That they will find the next 8 guardians." Glean said.

"Thank you Glean." Alena said.

"You are welcome. You should pate yourself on the back for you are the one who brought them together." Glen said.

"There is nothing much else we can do here. We need to get some sleep because we do have to still go to school tomorrow." Leroy said.

"You are right. They know to let us know what is going on when they send a guardian through the space of light." Jennifer said.

All the friends left for the night thinking and hoping that their friends are okay and will find the other guardians so that they can put a stop to this evil that has invaded their life, world, and unset the balance between dark and light. As Alena has started to walk home Leroy wanted to walk with her to make sure she would be okay with everything that has happened in the past few days.

"Are you okay?" Leroy asked.

"Yeah, why do you ask?" Alena said.

"You seem light years away from this place." Leroy said.

"I'm just worried about Sue and Joey that is all." Alena said.

Leroy walked Alena home in silent because there was so much tension between them that it could be cut with a knife. The most part was the fact that their friends are in unknown place and that things might not work out to their plan. All they could do right now is have faith and believe in Joey and Sue.

Meanwhile back on the Crystal Star of Fire Realm it was just started to get dawn and that is when Lola had woken everyone up. They knew that what was waiting for them was going to take everything they had.

"EVERYONE TIME TO GET UP!!!" Lola yelled.

Sue and Joey had jumped because they were in a deep sleep after the night events that had happened. They also knew that what they were going to face was not going to be an easy task. So, everyone had gotten up and started to get dress for those who had clothes to change into. Someone had offered Joey and Sue different clothes because what they were wearing would stand out like a sore thumb. So, the two accepted the clothes they were offered.

"Now listen up everyone. From here on out we will be in enemy territory which there might be fights on occasion so please be prepared before we head out. Everyone has one hour to eat, get dress, and what weapons they might need." Lola said.

"Lola what weapons do you use?" Sue asked.

"I use throwing stars, throwing knifes." Lola said.

"Oh, that is cool." Sue said.

"You can learn to use a weapon. If you want, I can teach you how to use a weapon of your choice." Lola said.

"Really, that would be so cool. I want to learn to use swords." Sue said.

"Okay I can teach you to use twin swords. I'm not that good at them but I can use them if the need arises. Joey, would you like to learn to use any type of weapons?" Lola asked.

"Yeah, if you are able could you teach me to use spears?" Joey asked.

"Of course, there is someone who can teach you how to use a spear or pike in my tribe and they are really good at it." Lola replied.

"That would be great." Joey said.

When everyone was ready by the hours' time was up. They started to head out of town. This was not a very big town they were in. As they started to walk Joey and Sue were given the weapons they had chosen to learn and would learn at night when they would break for camp. In the meantime, they needed to focus on keeping up with everyone most of all Lola.

"Listen everyone the castle is about three weeks walking from here. So, we are going to be moving fast and in times we will move slowly." Lola said.

As they started, she had pulled out a map to mark the way they would go. The first place they had planned to make it to be the great river Bear. So that was where they were going to set up camp for the night. It was a days' walk from the town. By the time they had reached halfway mark to the river it was high noon. The temps were getting warmer, and hotter. So, the group took a small break. Before they knew they were surrounded by the enemy.

"If it isn't the East Tribe of the Fire Realm." Someone had said from the shadows.

"Who goes there?" Lola demanded.

"Well young leader, I see you have new people. So, who are they?" The person said.

"That is none of your business." Lola said.

"Well, we will see about that. Our new leader is very interested in you, and I think he will want to know about those two new people you have with you. I am not sure why he is very interested in you, and I don't care if we keep you alive and kill the rest he won't care. I think we will let those two new people live as well seeing as they are not from here." General John Mash said.

"Who is this new leader you speak of?" Lola asked with angry.

"See you would have to defeat us before I tell you that." General John Mash said.

"That won't be too hard." Joey said coming up next to Lola.

"I agree." Sue said as well.

YOU DEAR SPEAK TOO TO ME; YOU LITTLE BRATS!" General John Mash yelled with angry.

"Yeah, we do." Joey and Sue said together.

"DON'T UNDERESMATE HIM YOU TWO." Lola yelled at them.

"He is stronger than you think. You don't have the skills to beat him by yourselves. But, together with me and everyone you can." Lola said.

As everyone stated to get into formation the enemy had them spilt up so that they could not work as a team. While Lola, Sue, and Joey were in one group with General John Mash the others were with his men. This enemy was going to stop them from going any further which was not a good thing. As they were trying to come up with a way to get out of this problem an attack came from nowhere. Before they knew it there was a big bag that had happened, and everyone was looking around to see where it came from. Before they knew it the enemy was on them.

"ATTACK!!!!" General John Mash yelled.

The three guardians were in a hand-to-hand combat with the enemy. Sue and Joey were not good at this because they never had to do a hand-to-hand combat with someone, they have learned self-defiance against another person, but this was way different.

"Whatever you do; don't let them get you. Watch out for John Mash attacks he has special powers over fire as well but has no control and when he goes berserk that is when the true powers of his comes out. So, whatever you do try to focus, if it comes down to it, we can use our powers as guardians and stop him." Lola told Joey and Sue this.

"In that case let's finish this before it gets worst." Joey said.

"I'm with you." Sue said.

"What do you plan on doing with no experience with hand-to-hand combat?" Lola asked.

"We need to use our powers to get out of this mess and help the others. Sue, you know what to do." Joey said.

"You got it." Sue said.

"LIGHT COME TO ME." Sue yelled.

"What is she going to do with a ball of light?" Lola asked.

"Just watch." Joey said.

"LIGHT FLASH BLIND THE ENEMY!!!" Sue yelled.

Sue releases the ball of light the enemy did not know what hit them or why they can't see. So as this happened it helped the other to fight back and reform the formation to take on General John Mash.

"What do you plan to do next?" Lola asked.

"It is time to show us what you have in powers." Joey told her.

"Okay you asked for it." Lola said laughing.

"FIRE COME TO ME!!" Lola yelled.

As the fire appeared she turned the fire into rings and combined her fire powers and her throwing stars together to form a throwing star with fire. It hit the enemy and when General John Mash was able to get his sight back, he was mad and then became berserk.

"HOW DARE YOU DO THIS TO US?" General John Mash yelled.

"DARK FIREBOMBS RAIN DOWN ON THEM!!!!" General John Mash yelled.

"Now it is my turn." Joey said with a smile.

"I CALL YOU WATER DRAGON COME TO ME!!" Joey yelled.

As the water dragon appeared Joey had summoned it to get rid of the dark firebombs.

"WATER DRAGON WE NEED WATER BOMBS!!" Joey yelled.

As the water bombs hit the dark firebombs it all turned into steam and when this happened the dark firebombs had disappeared. General John Mash was still standing there soaking wet in disbelief that this could happen to his most powerful attack.

"WHO ARE YOU TWO?" General John yelled.

"We are the guardians of the Majestic Star Kingdom. I'm the guardian of the Crystal Star Summons, and this young land here is the guardian of the Crystal Star of Light and Travel. We came here looking for the next guardian which we have found. She is Lola guardian of the Crystal Star of Fire she is one of the guardians and part of the court to the

Majestic Star Kingdom which will help us find our beloved star princess. the Majestic Star Kingdom can be reborn to our prince and princess." Joey told him.

"RETREAT FOR NOW. GUARDIAN OF SUMMONS I WILL BE BACK FOR YOUR HEAD!!" General John yelled at Joey.

As the enemy had fled to the headquarters of the enemy all everyone could do was stair at Joey and Sue. Even Lola seemed to be surprised by this change of events in her world and life. What Joey and Sue did not expect was that the people did not turn from them but clapped for them because this must have been a good sign to them all.

"Please tell who you are really?" Lola asked them

"We will tell you what you want to know after we get where we are going." Joey said.

"I have heard of this Majestic Star Kingdom; it was story that my adopted parents always told me about when I was little." Lola said.

"We will talk when we get where we are going, okay." Sue said.

"Okay, but you promise that you will tell me everything I want to know and answer my question you two." Lola asked.

"Yes." Joey and Sue said together.

As the conversion had stopped now so that they could start walking to where they were going. As the day passed, they were almost to the river which will be the place they set up camp for the night. Sue and Joey kept looking at the place they were in and still could not see how this beautiful realm could be so stunning with all the fighting going on. Most of all what was bugging the two friends was what General John Mash had said about a new leader of their tribe from the north which is also the direction of the Fire Realm Castle. As they all kept walking, they finally reach the river Bear and started to set up camp. After everyone had set up their tents, they all sat down to eat and that is when Lola started her questioning of Joey and Sue.

"So, tell me about the star princess and the prince." Lola asked.

"The prince has been found, but before we start with that you need to tell us what you know about the Majestic Star Kingdom." Joey said.

"Okay, I will tell you the story that my parents told me." Lola said.

Everyone sat around the campfire to listen to the story she was about to tell.

Chapter 3

"The story goes back about a thousand years ago. When there was the most beautiful Majestic Star Kingdom; that everyone wanted to be a part of. So, the story of this kingdom was that the most beautiful Queen and her handsome King had ruled for many years. Then the Queen had become pageant with the next heir to the throne. The people of the kingdom were so happy that finally the Queen and King would have a son or daughter. The King was well friends with the Elemental Realm King, which the king, and his queen had a son which was 4 years old when the news was sent that the Queen of the Majestic Star Kingdom was going to have a baby.

Both kings got together one day and had talked if the baby was a girl, then the young prince of the Elemental Crystal Star Realm would marry her one day. So, the Crystal Star Realms all came together to welcome the new baby when the time came. It was the most wonderful time of peace. Every realm was happy that the Majestic Star Kingdom would now have an heir to the throne. Then the time came that the baby was due to be born. The baby was born on March 15, and it turned out that the baby was a girl so beautiful that she had passed her mother's beauty which was fine with the Queen and King of the Majestic Star Kingdom. Every realm had cheered and celebrated the birth of the baby girl. She would grow to be so beautiful that no one would be able to look away. She would also be the most powerful of the realms. She would be able to use powers far beyond that of her parents.

Queen Daisy and King Devon were the proudest parents and the happiest of the realms that they finally had a daughter that will one day rule and by her side the strongest of princes would help become the next queen of the Majestic Star Kingdom and they would rule over the kingdom with their court at their sides. As the star princess grew, she had the most beautiful hair that could not be missed she had hair the color of a raven's feather, skin as dark as an Indian, and she was the kindest person in all the realms. Then one day the peace was shattered by a dark evil and a dark kingdom that Queen Daisy and King Devon was forced to send their beloved daughter, the prince from the Elemental Crystal Star Realm, and their court a thousand years into the future hoping there would be peace there." Lola had finished the story.

"So, from the story I know who the prince is because he has been noticed by the Dark Kingdom

Zodiac, which is Leroy who is a guardian of the Crystal Star of the Elemental Realm. He can use all the elements. Then there is the guardian of the Crystal Star of Water and Ice Realm Alena." Joey said.

"What you are telling me is there are more guardians out there beside the two you." Lola asked.

"Yes, there are 12 guardians in all that is including the prince and princess. We know of the prince, but we still need to find the star princess." Sue said.

"So, what you are saying is that the Majestic Star Kingdom does exist, and each guardian was sent back to their own realms a thousand years into the future and if the Dark Kingdom Zodiac was to attack again or awaken then the star princess would be able to stop them." Lola asked.

"Yes, and you catch on quick." Joey said with a smile.

"Thanks, so do you know who the star princess might be we are looking for?" Lola asked.

"No, we don't have a clue. It could be any of us girls. As it stands there are other guardians that yet need to be found." Sue replied.

"We have a hell of a time trying to find this star princess so that we could have peace again." Lola said.

"Yeah, so you are on board about being a guardian to help us?" Joey asked her.

"You got it bud." Lola said with a smile and laugh.

"That is cool Lola, welcome to the team. So, you know; when we are done here in this realm; I will send you back to the Crystal Star of Water and Ice, were you will meet our prince, and the guardian of water and ice. They are Leroy Addams, and Alena Patches. Both are the same age as you and me." Sue said.

"That sounds like it will be a long time before I reach them." Lola replied.

"No, you mistaken it would only take you a few minutes, because I will open up a portal of light which we are the only ones who will be able to go through." Sue said.

"Oh, I see what you mean." Lola said.

"Now that we have covered all that, we need to think of who this new enemy is. Any ideas?" Joey said.

"Your right. I have never run into General John Mash with so much power before. It is like someone, or something gave him a power boost." Lola said.

"I have an idea who it might be, but my question is how did they get here in the first place?" Sue said.

"I think you might me right cuz, which would make a lot of sense." Joey said.

"What are you two thinking, could you clue me in please." Lola asked.

"We think that it is in no doubt the Dark Kingdom Zodiac. Which is out to keep the Majestic Star Kingdom from being rebuilt and reborn. It is also the reason the Majestic Star Kingdom was destroyed in the past." Joey said.

"The kingdom from my parents' story is true, and really does exist in this reality." Lola said with a grim look on her face.

"Yes, they are real, and their goal is to rule all." Sue said.

As the three guardians was talking way into the night, they had not slept at all before the group started to move out of their camping spot. Which would make them walk for the next few days without a break to at least cut the time down to get to the castle. It had already been a day since they left the town and started out on their journey to the Fire Castle were the guardians were hoping to find answers to how to find the other guardians' realms and send them back to the Crystal Star of Water and Ice where their friends were waiting for them to return. Joey and Sue knew there was going to be a lot to finding the last 7 guardians. As they are thinking about how, why, when, and where they were. Something happens; the group had felt like they were being pulled down to the ground.

"What is going on?" Sue yelled.

"It is a gravity barrier field." Lola said.

"What is that supposed to mean?" Sue asked.

"It means we have walked into enemy territory." Lola yelled back.

"How do we get out of it?" Joey piped in.

"I am not sure; do you have any ideas?" Lola yelled back.

"Not a clue." Joey said.

"Well, it would seem that the guardians have run out of tricks." A person said.

"Who is there?" Sue yelled.

"Well guardian of Light and Travel it would seem you don't have much of a memory." Strange person said.

"Memory, what am I supposed to remember?" Sue said.

"Well guardian of Light and Travel that is for you to figure out." Strange person said.

As Sue was trying to think of the man's voice, she knew the voice but could not figure out who it was. She knew that she heard the voice before, but her mind was drawing a blank. If she can't figure out whose voice that is then she would be responsible for everyone getting caught. She knows that she has heard the voice before. Then it hits her like a train going 50 mph which is very fast.

"The Dark Prince Jordan, how did you find us two guardians? I see that you can't get to Alena anymore." Sue said.

"It took you long enough guardian of light and travel. Which that is saying something that you are a true blonde." Dark Prince Jordan started to laugh.

"It may take me long to figure out who you are, but I did; so that is saying blondes are very smart. It also goes to show that I can think on my feet and when my friends and me are in trouble." Sue replied with a smirk.

"Is that you did. We rule this realm now and you and the rest will go no further than this." Dark Prince Jordan said.

"Whatever you say. You will not stop us here we will figure this out we always do. When we do you better be scared because we are coming for you and your Dark Kingdom." Sue said with angry.

"I am with her. Last I checked we defeated you once before." Joey said.

"I summon the Dragon of Ice." Joey Called.

"This might help if we can overpower the gravity with our powers then we can get out of this barrier and wipe the floor with his damned face." Lola yelled.

"I am with you." Sue said.

"I call light to me." Sue called.

"I call fire to me." Lola said.

As the three guardians put all their power into the barrier it broke as the barrier broke the Dark Prince disappeared and they knew this would not be the last time they see him. As they noticed they were maybe two days away from the castle and they wanted to get out of this area before anything else happened. So, they group started to head out of the area where they were near the dark forest which would drain their powers and their will. So, the group went the long way around. Which was near a cave that was filled with warm light? So, the groups choose to stay in this cave which was outside of the dark forest that surrounds the castle. It also had three tunnels that went in three different directions the center, right, and the left tunnel. Each group of three would take a tunnel to find a way through the dark forest.

"We will have to find the safest route into the dark forest to get to the castle." Lola said.

"What do you mean?" Joey asked.

"I mean we will have to go through the forest somehow to get to the castle because that is where we need to go." Lola said.

"What you mean is that unless we can find another route into the castle, we would have to go through the dark forest which could be filled with enemies around each corner." Sue replied.

"That is very right Sue." Lola said.

"Okay then let us explore this cave in groups of three. I think that each of us guardians should take a group so that we can spread out our power and help the others to protect this realm." Joey said.

"We agree with you." Sue and Lola said together and started to laugh.

"The next question is who will take the first group and let the others rest and sleep if it is needed." Joey said.

"I will take the first watch, group, and tour the cave the best I can. I think that because this is my realm, and I am responsible for it." Lola said.

"That is fine with us. Who will you take with you?" Joey asked.

"I will take my right-hand man Jerry Tower which he is the best in weapons. The second would be David James because he is the best guide there is in the group. This will be my group of three and the other that don't go with you two can stay and be on watch. So, who are you going to take Sue and Joey?" Lola asked.

"For me I want to take Nicole Johnson because she is the best at long range fright and is a master bow user, my second choice is Bryan Henry because he is your master of martial arts. This is my group of three." Sue said.

"Ask for me I want to take along is for my first would have to be Nelson Carter because he is good at watching someone's back also, he is one of the best at marking out traps and can track the enemy very well if there is any here, and for my second I want to take Maria Johnson which is the sister of Nicole Johnson, and she is also great with a bow but can also do martial arts close up. This is my group of three." Joey said.

"Then it is settled we have our groups and then we need to get started because if we stay here to long then there is a chance that the enemy could come back." Lola said.

As the friends started to plan how they were going to do this in the next 16 hours, which is how much time they had before dawn. That is how long it might take to try and find a way through the dark forest without going through the forest. So, Lola and her group were going first which they chose to take the left side of the cave, Joey took the right tunnel but before he took the tunnel he ran over to Lola and kissed her on her ruby red lips which had made her smile from ear to ear. Sue's month had dropped and could not believe he would do that to her best friend, and before she had taken the center tunnel, she was going to give her cousin a peace of her mind before going down her tunnel.

"What was that for?" Lola asked.

"It was for luck, and I want you to promise me that you will come back safe and sound. If you run into trouble, then run away don't fight without me or Sue there with you. I know how bullheaded a redhead can be. I want you to know that you light the fire in my soul I mean more than any woman I have ever been with, except one but she was more into another guy than me, she is a very wonderful person and I'm glad that she is into someone else. I have never meet any one like you. Not a single person can touch my soul like you did when we first met." Joey said.

"WOW!" Lola said.

"Good luck Lola and be careful." Sue said.

Joey had looked at Sue and noticed she was giving him the evil eyes he had never seen this on his cousin which meant she was about to blow her top on him. He looked at Sue to make sure that she wasn't really going to blow her top at him. She seemed to claim down a little bit which is a really great thing, cause he didn't need his cousin losing her temper right now.

"Listen Sue before you say anything Alena and I are not together anymore which I am free to feel for someone that cares for me." Joey said.

"Alena did care for your ass whole, she cared about you no matter whether she has feelings for someone else." Sue said with angry.

"That is the point, Sue; she has feelings for Leroy Addams which is why she needed to be freed from me. Then the dumbass got cold feet after seeing a picture a girl that he thought he knew." Joey said.

"I DON'T CARE; IF YOU HURT HER IN ANY WAY FOR ANY REASON YOU WILL DEAL WITH ME." Sue yelled.

"Please claim down. I don't plan on hurting Alena in anyway which that is saying something because I still care for her, but not the way I care for Lola. I care about Alena as a really good friend not a girlfriend in that sense." Joey pleaded.

"Fine for now I will let it go. Just so you know when you get a chance you better tell Alena about you and Lola." Sue said.

"Okay." Joey said.

After their little argument Joey had started down the left tunnel with his group of three. He had notice that there were crystals in the walls of the cave which would explain why there was a soft and warm light coming from the cave, but he also notices that the crystals had glowed different colors and one caught his eye which was the color of purple. He didn't know why this one crystal had caught his eye, but it did. So, as he is walking along one of the guards had stopped and pulled out his weapon it was Nelson who could spot a trap from miles away.

"What is it, Nelson?" Joey asked

"Sir there are many traps and enemies up ahead which is going to give us a problem." Nelson said.

"Is there a way to get around the traps and enemy?" Joey asked.

"Yes, sir there is a way, but we will still need to fight our way through to the other side." Nelson said.

"What do we need to do?" Joey asked.

"I will need help from Maria and her bow." Nelson said.

"What do you need Nelson?" Maria said.

"Need to know can you hit that lavage over there to release the traps and if able can you try and take out some of those giant spiders that is blocking our way." Nelson asked.

"You got it." Maria said.

As Maria took aim with her bow, she knew that she only got one hit for the lavage and then start firing arrows at the giant spiders. After the lavage releases the traps the other two would have to start backing her up only if to make it out of this mess alive and get back to their friends.

"Get ready you two." Maria said.

"You got it." Nelson said.

"I got your back Maria and Nelson. I am going to summon my dragon of lighting." Joey said.

"Okay he goes nothing." Maria said.

"I summon the lighting dragon." Joey called.

"I have my gloves on and have my sword in hand." Nelson said.

As the arrow hit the lavage and releasing all the traps and she started to fire arrows at each giant spider that started coming their way along with Joey, and Nelson which was started to take out the giant spiders and she started to run across the bridge to the other side of the tunnel and saw that there was a turn they would have to take which was still filled with giant spiders and giant scorpions. As Nelson and Joey cross the bridge Nelson breaks the bridge so that the giant spiders fell into the pit under them. As they reached Maria, they had notice she stopped moving.

"Maria what is it?" Nelson asked.

"We have three problems which start with we have to make a turn here, and on this side, we are not just dealing with giant spiders, but also giant scorpions. My question to you is that how are we going to get back across the bridge if it is not there anymore?" Maria said.

"Well, the answer to your question is that I can fly us across on one of my dragons that I can summon." Joey answered.

"Okay that does answer my first question. Now for my second question is how are we going to get passed these bugs?" Maria asked.

"We fight our way across. That is the only way we are going to get passed these insects." Nelson said.

As the three fight their way across the next part of the tunnel they realize it was a dead end and need to get back to the others. Joey started to worry about Lola and Sue. As they reached the broken bridge that Nelson had broken; Joey had to summon his light dragon so that the three friends could get back to the others.

"Light Dragon I summon you." Joey called forth.

They all claimed on the back of the Light Dragon so they could fly across the bridge. As they fly across the bridge, they notice that it was getting darker, and things started to get colder as well. They started to get sleepy because of the cold they are feeling.

Lola had spilt up from the others, so Joey and Sue had to find her in the other tunnel that she went down. Praying that she is okay and not harmed but fighting for her life and wouldn't go down so easily seen as she is the guardian of the Fire Realm.

Chapter 4

❖─◆─○─◆─❖

$\mathcal{M}$eanwhile as Lola had started down the right tunnel after getting kissed by Joey. She could not help but keep smiling and as she was thinking about the kiss she ran into the back of David. Then she notices that the walls were shining like stars and crystals. Then as she looked closer, she notices the things she thought were stars turned out to be crystals. Then she saw it a crystal that looked red, and it really shined as she got near it.

"David where are we?" Lola asked.

"I am not sure, but it looks like the cave we came into was a crystal cave which was giving off that soft glow and warmth." David answer.

"Well, no matter where we are we have guest." Jerry said.

"What do you mean we have guest Jerry?" Lola asked.

"We just walked into a giant spider den." Jerry said.

As Lola walked up to Jerry, she saw what he was taking about. As she was standing there, she could not keep the promise to Joey all she could do was fight her way through because she needed to find a way out of the cave, and past the dark forest because she never wants to enter that evil, dark, place again; because she had damn near lost herself in there when she was younger. If it wasn't for her father, she most likely would have lost her life, or became a general for the Dark Kingdom Zodiac. Which she did not want. Next to her came David with his two draggers out, Jerry had pulled out his spear, and Lola called fire to her. As three friends fought their way through the giant spiders, they notice that there was a "T" up ahead and she needed to know which way to go, so she chooses to go right but something or someone whispered that is the wrong way go left. As they turned left, they ran into more problems on top of the giant spiders, giant ants, and giant scorpions, there was traps all over the place. As they kept going, they fought to get out and as they came to the end of the tunnel, she had notice light up ahead.

"Is that a way out of here?" Lola asked.

"It looks like it might be. We need to check it out." David said.

"Then let us go and check it out." Lola said.

"Agreed." Jerry and David said together.

As they got closer to the end of the tunnel they came out of the tunnel and found that they were on the other said of the dark forest and right there was the Fire Castle. Which had knocked down their time by half, they needed to get back to tell the others. This was the way to get to the castle without going through the dark forest. Which was what Lola truly wanted because of the horror she felt in the dark forest that one time, she didn't need or want her friends to feel it. She finally had true friends and was about have a few more when she goes to the Water and Ice Crystal Star Realm where two guardians were still waiting on news from their friends.

"We need to get back to the others and let them know we found another way through." Lola said.

"Then let us go." Jerry said.

So, the three made their way back to the others and Lola was started to worry about Sue and Joey. All she was hoping that they would be okay because she didn't want to be alone ever again. Now she might even have a guy that is into her, and she started to think about the kiss which had touched her soul as if he was met for her. She has never felt this before and wanted it to stay and keep her going to her friends. Then she notices that he could be her soul mate which would most likely be cool. She wanted to feel that way for a very long time. This is what she always wanted and most of all she wanted to have friends who would accept her for her. As the three got back to the beginning of the tunnel they ran into Joey and his group, and they were looking down the center tunnel hoping Sue would appear soon. She never came out, Joey wanted to go after her, but Lola stopped him.

"Joey please give her a chance. I also need to let you and the others know that we had found a way out that would cut our time down by at least half a day." Lola said.

"Okay. Come here." Joey said.

As she came near him; he grabbed her and pulled her into a hug, and he bent down and kissed and did not want to let her go at all. When they kissed it was like the world had stopped spinning, and time had stopped just for them. When they finally pulled apart from each other they just stood there smiling at each other and just kept holding on as if this would be their last time to be together and that they would have to go their own ways soon.

"I never want this feeling to stop when I am near you." Lola said.

"I would have to agree with you. Let us head back to the opening of the cave where everyone is waiting and if Sue don't come back in the next four hours, then we are going to find her." Joey said.

"Okay. But I would like to tell you more about me if you will listen to me, please." Lola asked.

"I will listen to you from one end of the universe to the other. I like the sound of your voice." Joey said.

Lola started to blush and then she just stood on her tippy toes to kiss him. Joey lends down and he kissed her like it was the last time ever. As they started to walk near the entrance of the crystal cave, she was happy to be a part of something so special, and good. So, they sat down near the fire that must have been started after they went to check the cave out. As they sat down, she was happy to be next to him. As well as how there is a lot, she needed to tell him about herself. What she was worried about was that will he still want her, and Sue still want to be her friend. So, as they sat down, she started to speak.

"Joey there is a few things I want you to know about me and I want Sue to know as well." Lola said.

"What is it? You can tell me, and you can trust both Sue and me." Joey said.

"Okay. Well, you should know that when I was younger, I never had friends like Sue and you. Most of all know guy would look my way or even take a second look. Also, I felt that I was an outcast because of my ability to use fire. So, when growing up I made people very sacred of me. So, to be honest I needed you to know that if you had not agreed to help us, I was going to make you." Lola said with a sad face.

"Well first you can't force someone to do as you wish that would not make you any better than the Dark Kingdom Zodiac who had taken over your realm by force. Second, we saw the goodness in your heart the first time you spoke to us. Third if you didn't have friends then why is everyone willing to help you now?" Joey asked her.

"They follow me because I forced them and because I was mean to them all." Lola said.

"I am sorry for interrupting; buy my lady you are very wrong in that. We follow you because we know you have a pure heart, and that you would sacrifice yourself for us as we would do for you." Nelson said.

"Nelson, don't I scare you? Why would you follow a person like me?" Lola asked.

"We follow you because you are our Fire Princess, and you have such a really good, pure heart. Also, we know you caused a lot of problems for us in the past, but we overlooked them because we cared about you." Nelson said.

As Lola was sitting there, she started to cry and could feel all the love around her. She could not believe that these people all cared for her. Also, she realized then that she has had friends all long.

As Sue's group of three had started down the center tunnel hoping to at least find a way around this dark forest. She knew that it would not be easy, also that it could take them a long time just to find a way out. As the three starts down the tunnel a sudden guest of wind had come near as if the fire realm was no longer a part of the tunnel, but they knew better. As they continue down the tunnel, they hear moving ahead of them. As they reach a fork in the road something told Sue to take the right path and that is what they did. As they come around the bind, they run into some major big spiders that seemed to have made the crystal cave their home. So, they would have to proceed with caution which would not be easy because it was a very narrow path. As they a pouch the giant spider's layer they notice that they spiders were blocking their way.

"The only way through here is down this past which I have no clue where it lends." Bryan said.

"What do you mean? Is there any way around them without fighting?" Sue asked.

"No, am afraid not." Bryan said.

"Okay, Nicole can you use your bow skills to at least take some down and I can use my light power to help fight." Sue said.

"You got it boss." Nicole said with a laugh, which was not at all a really good time to be joking around but she wanted to lighten up everyone's mood.

As Nicole first placed her arrow on her bow and let it fly. It hit the target which was a good thing because the giant spiders were heading for them.

"Light rings come to me." Sue yelled

As Sue had gathered light into her hands, Bryan was putting on his fighting gloves and was ready for a fight. As arrows flew, light rings cycled around the arrows as the arrows hit the giant spiders, and Bryan used his power punch to split the ground to seed the giant spiders to their death the path was finally clear enough to get though. As the group kept walking, they realized there was a soft green glow coming from up ahead of them. Sue had summoned her light power again to light their way through the dark path to the green light. As they a pouch the giant green crystal Sue notice that it was the size of a mirror then as her light had hit something happened, the crystal started to glow and then a door opened to another realm as she could tell. The others were not sure what it was.

"Sue what is this?" Bryan asked.

"It is a portal to the Crystal Realm of Wind." Sue said.

"How do you know that?" Nicole asked.

"Because I can see a green forest which looks like the Rain Forest in the Crystal Realm of Water and Ice, but more cared for." Sue said.

"OH!!" Bryan and Nicole said together.

As Sue looked on, she could not help but feel the warmth of another guardian in this realm. They needed to get back to the others so she could let Joey and Lola know that she had found a way to the next guardian.

"Let us head back to our friends and inform them of what we have found." Sue said.

"Okay you got it." Bryan said.

The three guardians head back down the path they came from and knew that they would have to find a way across the crack in the ground Bryan put there. As they were reaching the end of their path something came out of the shadows and attacked them. Before Sue could send her light attack at the insect they were caught. SO, she had sent a light to Joey and Lola hoping they knew what it met.

As the light had few through the air it got to Joey and Lola, and everyone started to scream because they thought it was an attack by the enemy, so Joey and Lola had span around and before they knew it the light ball let out a low "HELP" which met that Sue, and her group were in major trouble.

"That was Sue!" Lola yelled.

"That means she and her group are in major trouble." Joey said.

"Lets' go save them." Lola said.

"I agree with you." Joey said.

As they had chosen to save their friends the light ball had flew right down the center tunnel, and they followed right behind it. As they reach the crack in the ground, they notice a giant spider had them wrapped in a web and they could not move. "Maria, can you use your bow to cut the web around our friends while the rest of us fight the ones guarding it?" Joey asked.

"I am already ahead of you sir." Maria said.

As Maria had release her arrow it cut though the web and their friends fell to the ground. Sur got up mad as hell and called her powers of light to her and as she did this her power lite the whole cave up making it shine as if increasing her powers, a thousand times. She released her light balls on the giant spiders turning them to dust just like the sun rays does. Then after releasing her powers, she falls to the ground unconscious. Bryan had picked her up and was going to carry her rest of the way.

"Hey buddy is there any way you can get us out of here?" Bryan asked Joey.

"Hold on I am coming we can fly on the back of one of my dragons." Joey yelled back.

"Cool that works for me." Nicole said with a smile.

"I summon you light dragon we need your help." Joey called.

As the light dragon appeared he climbed on her back and flew across the crack in the ground and picked up the others. As they went back across Sue was out cold and need rest before they could travel, good thing they still had about 5 hours before dawn so she could rest. The whole group of nine headed back to the entrance to the cave with Bryan carrying Sue. Nicole had filled everyone in on the portal to the Wind Realm in the back of the cave. Lola filled them in about a way out of the cave to the right tunnel she had taken.

Chapter 5

As Sue had been out for a few hours by overusing her powers while she sleeps; the others make plans to move forward through the cave. The group had chosen to leave after Sue wakes up. As she slept the others started to pack up camp and as she started to come to. She had waked up and notices that everyone was trying to get their things together as well as to move out.

"What is going on?" Sue asked.

"We found a way into the castle without going through the dark forest." Lola said to Sue.

"She is awake everyone." Lola yelled over the crowd.

Everyone looked at her and kept working to get ready to head out.

"What is going on?" Sue asked again.

"Dear cousin you finally woke up. You overused your powers, also Lola had found a way around the dark forest through the crystal cave. So, we are packing up and moving through the cave to get to the Fire Realm Castle." Joey said.

"Okay I get what is happening." Sue said.

So, she got on her feet to help pack the camp up. As the others start to move so did, she. As they reached the area were they needed to go and reach the opening to the castle grounds? Lola had explained what they need to go next. As they a pouch the path to the right she shows them the way to the castle. The group made it to the end of the tunnel. As they walked out of the tunnel the dark forest was on the other side of the castle. The castle was tall, dark grey, with a hint of red in the blocks, it had picks on all four corners, and the doorway to the grand hall was as big as a building. So, the whole group walked into the castle.

"Welcome to the Fire Realm Castle guardians." Dark Prince Jordan said.

"What are you doing in this castle?" Lola said.

"Well guardian of fire your realm is ours." Dark Prince Jordan.

"It will never be yours as long as I am still got breathe in my lungs, my heart pounding, and I can still move. We will stop you." Lola yelled.

"You know guardian I will have to take your word on it. You do know I had kidnapped one of you and she could not keep me from taking control." Prince Jordan said.

"You lie. She was taken by your father, and she stopped you in your tracks. I can see you still have the hot for Alena." Sue said.

"Don't worry guardian of light I have not forgotten what you all did to keep her from becoming mine for good. Also, I still can get my hands on her if I want to." Prince Jordan said.

"You could try but she is not alone she has Leroy, Jennifer, and Glen there to protect her from the likes of you." Joey said.

"Well, we will see about that. If you can reach the throne room before night fall, I will leave this realm unharmed." Prince Jordan said.

"How can we believe the likes of you?" Lola yelled.

"You don't know for certain. You are just going to have to try, it will not be easy." Prince Jordan said.

"I call further the Dark Phoenix." Prince Jordan yelled.

"Now what do we do?" Lola yelled.

"We fight." Joey said.

"Summon the light dragon." Joey yelled.

"I call light to me." Sue yelled.

"Leave this to us." Joey yelled at Lola.

"Go! Only you can get what we need. We also need to get to the portal to the wind realm." Sue yelled

"All right." Lola yelled.

As Lola ran with her group only six stayed behind to help Joey and Sue to fight the Dark Phoenix. As they reach the throne room, Lola could not believe what she was looking at. The Dark Prince was sitting in her biological father's throne chair. As she is looking at the Dark Prince in a case to the right of the throne room was a crown with the flame symbol on it and another one that had a moon and star forge in it. Lola knew she needed to get both crowns but getting past the Dark Prince was not going to be easy. As they start in the fighting Lola notice that the Dark Prince was a lot quicker than she thought.

"What are you going to do?" Prince Jordan said.

"We will stop you here." Lola said.

"You can try." Prince Jordan said.

"Then we will help her." Joey said while running up to Lola's side.

"Your dark phoenix disappeared into the night, back to your dark realm." Sue said.

"Well then this is a problem. I will let you go for now." Price Jordan said.

As the Prince disappeared through a dark smoke screen back to the Dark Kingdom Zodiac. So, Lola walked over to the Fire Crown and touched her hand on it, and it opened. She pulled out the crown and handed it to Nicole Johnson and Jerry Tower. Then she walked over to the other case but when she touched it. It would not open at her touch.

"I don't understand why this won't open." Lola said.

"Then let us try together." Sue said.

So, all three guardians touched the case and it opened. Joey took out the crown and put into his bag for safe keeping.

"What am I supposed to do with this crown it belongs to you, my lady?" Nicole asked.

"For now, I want you two to act in my place over our realm and keeping it safe until I can return." Lola said.

"We will do our best my lady." Jerry said.

"I leave everything in both your capable hands. We need to head to that wind portal you found Sue." Lola said.

"Yes, we do, I don't know how long it will remain open." Sue said.

"Then we need to go." Joey said.

As the friends said goodbye to their friends, they headed back through the crystal cave and down the center tunnel. Joey had summoned a dragon for them to get over the crack in the ground and then they head for the green crystal and the portal to the wind realm. As they a pouched the portal Lola seemed sad to be leaving her home, but something told it was the right thing to do. As the three guardians went through the portal and landed in a forest that smelled of rain forest.

Crystal Star of
the Wind Realm

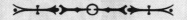

Chapter 6

The forest was very humid, wet, and above all very beautiful. The guardians started to walk through the forest and taking in all the scenes they could see. As they walked through the forest it started to get foggy and hard to see.

"What is going on, it was clear a little while ago." Sue asked.

"It seems that maybe we had walked into something, or it could just be the stream coming off the water fall nearby." Lola said.

"Where did you get that from?" Joey asked.

"I can hear it in the desistence." Lola said with a smirk.

"Oh. I hear it now." Joey said.

"DUH, I have been hearing it for a while now." Sue said.

As they continued to walk, they started to feel as if they were being watched. It was as if they had stepped into a horror film. So, they continued into the forest, the deeper they go the foggier it got. As they walked it seemed as if day had turned into night, things started to get dark for the guardians it was as if they were started to fall asleep in this deep forest. It was as wind had taken over them and they passed out.

When they finally came too, they were inside of a hut made of trees and grass. They didn't understand why they were here and what is going on.

"Welcome to the Forest of Jade, this forest can play tricks on your mind, and the minute you walk in." The odd person said.

"Did you help us out?" Sue asked.

"Yes, I saw that you three had passed out due to the humidity in the forest. My name is Richard Springer, please call me Rich." Rich said.

"It is nice to meet you. These are my friends Joey, Lola, and you can call me Sue." Sue said.

"It is nice to meet all of you. So, what are you doing in the forest? Were you all looking for something or someone?" Rich asked.

"Yeah, we are looking for someone. We just don't know where to start looking. We also didn't suspect that we would pass out due to the heat." Lola said.

"So do you know this person?" Rich asked

"No, we just know that we need to get to the castle of this realm." Sue said.

"Well, you should know that the castle is being overrun by dangerous people, and that if we go near it the people start to act different." Rich said.

"It sounds like you guys are having some problems. So, you know what this danger is?" Joey asked

"Yeah, they call themselves the Dark Zodiac. I have heard legends about such darkness, but I have never seen it in my life until just recently." Rich said.

"It would seem that the Dark Kingdom Zodiac's reach is further than anticipated." Sue said.

"Yeah!" Lola and Joey said together.

"Do you know of this darkness? Have you heard of it before?" Rich asked.

"Let me put it in terms like this: The Dark Kingdom Zodiac has attacked the Fire Realm, Water and Ice Realm, Summons Realm, The Wind Realm, and all the other realms. It destroyed a very special kingdom called The Majestic Star Kingdom which had a very loving Queen and King, not only that but the heir to the throne of this kingdom the Star Princess and the Prince of the Element Realm have been lost sue to the Dark Kingdom Zodiac. They are very scary and dangerous for anyone to try and get near them." Joey said.

"I have heard legends of The Majestic Star Kingdom; it is an old story passed down through the generations. My parents told me the story when I was young, and I became very interested in this kingdom and went to a temple not far from the village." Rich asked.

"Is it possible that you can show us the temple?" Lola asked.

"Yeah, I can show it to you. It is about a two day walk from here." Rich said.

"Cool then let us go." Sue said.

"Before we go you need to eat, rest, and clean up a little bit. I will lead you to the temple of Emerald." Rich said.

The four ate, got cleaned up, and rested. They had planned to head out at first light so they could get a good start to the temple. Richard Springer is 6'4" tall, dark mocha skin tone, long brown hair, and eyes the color of Jade. When they woke up the next morning it seemed to be even more foggy than it was in the afternoon when they first appeared in the Wind Realm. As the guardians and their new friend was getting dressed for their journey out into the wild of the Forest of Jade that things seem to be very uneasy to them. They wanted to know more than avoiding trouble with the Dark kingdom Zodiac and remain undetected to them so they can move quickly without a fight at every corner like it has been. They knew it was a matter of time before they knew all three guardians are here in this realm as well. They were wondering how long the Dark Kingdom has been in this realm, because it seems that there is no guardian here to protect these people from their darkness.

"Rich how long has the Dark Kingdom Zodiac been here?" Sue asked.

"I am not sure how long, because they were here when I was born, so am assuming that they have been in the wind realm as you all call it for very long time. My grandparents said they remember a time when there was peace when our true king and queen ruled but was taken over by wanting power, so they agreed to the be part of the Dark Kingdom Zodiac, but they were killed about 10 years ago and the Dark Kingdom took overruling our lands." Rich said.

"Oh, they are trying to rule all the realms. So, I think that we are going to see this wherever we go from here on out." Joey said.

"Yeah, you are right." Sue said.

"Well, we need to get going if we want to make it at least halfway to the temple of Emerald. So, you know that when you enter the forest of Jade always beware of where you are because we don't need you all to pass out again." Rich said.

"I think that we will be fine because I bodies had a chance to rest and refuel." Lola said.

"I agree with you, I think now we will be able to handle the humid from here on out." Sue said.

"Good, then let us move quickly before the Dark Kingdom notices anything." Rich said.

The group head out into the forest of Jade with their surroundings in mind. They also notice they could change for the weather and moving quickly as they can in the forest. The village was very small with huts as homes because of it being so hot in the forest. The three guardians could see flowers of all colors, shapes, and sizes. Some flowers they have never had a chance to look at even in their own mine. This place was very pretty; too bad the Dark Kingdom Zodiac had its claws in it already for the past 10 years. The three guardians could feel the power of the Dark Kingdom as they move through the forest. They knew it would be any time they notice their powers as well. As the guardians was looking around, they notice some things where no different than those they have seen in books. It was as if the writer had been here before, but they were not aware of the realms being connected. Sue could open a portal anywhere if she knew what it looked like. As the group kept walking in the shadow of the trees for shade from the blazing sun it felt cooler than it did when they first step into the Wind Realm. As they walked the started to wonder about whom Rich was and how he grew up in a small village with the interest in the Temple of Emerald.

"Rich can you tell us about yourself?" Sue asked.

"Yeah, it would pass time by. What do you want to know?" Rich said.

"Well, who are your parents?" Sue asked.

"I never got to know my mother because she passed away after childbirth. My father died about 10 years ago around the same time the Darkness came to this world." Rich said.

"Oh; sorry to hear that. Do you have any family left?" Sue asked.

"No, I am the only one left out of my family." Rich said.

"How did your father die 10 years ago?" Lola asked.

"He died saving me from my Great Aunt and Great Uncle who ruled this realm. My father was next in line for the crown because my aunt and uncle could not have children. So, I have royal blood running through my veins but when they agreed to work with the Dark Kingdom Zodiac and tried to kill my father and me. That is when my father gave his life for me. I have been on my own every sense." Rich said.

"How old are you?" Sue asked.

"I am 17 years old. The village people took me in as one of their own and I worked for everything I have. The reason for that was because my father was good friends with the Chef of the village." Rich said.

"WOW! You are a year older than us." Joey said.

As the group walked and kept talking about how the Dark Kingdom Zodiac took overruling the realm and how Rich survived all these years without any real family to help him. The three guardians were wondering who the guardian of the Crystal Star of Wind was. They did not sense any powers when they enter the realm from the beginning and was wondering if there was even a guardian to this realm anymore. As they walked through the forest, they started to sense something evil in the air.

"Hold on something is here and it doesn't belong here." Rich said.

As Rich held out his hand to stop the three guardians from walking any further, they started to sense the evil of the Dark Kingdom Zodiac.

"Rich this is not what you think it is. It is the Dark Kingdom Zodiac. We sense when they are near to us because we are reborn guardians of the Majestic Star Kingdom." Joey said.

"What is a guardian?" Rich said.

"They are sworn to protect the star princess and the prince which is to rule the Majestic Star Kingdom. We as guardians help them in ruling the kingdom by keeping the peace among all the Crystal Star Realms." Sue said.

"I see so you are like bodyguards for the kingdom." Rich said.

"Yeah, but it is more than that. We are also friends with each other, and we care, and are pure at heart, just like you." Lola said.

"Well, I am no guardian because I have no powers to speak of." Rich said.

"Well, there has to be a guardian on this realm." Joey said.

"Whoever it is I don't know. Is that that you are looking for?" Rich asked.

"Yes, we are also looking for a way to the next realm and what realm that might be." Sue said.

They were wondering when the attack will come from the Dark Kingdom Zodiac. As they are walking through the forest of Jade as things started to go wrong. The path was over running by plants, and some what they could see this is a dark spell the Dark Kingdom Zodiac has cast to keep the people from going any further to the temple.

"It would seem we have some lost kittens." Mystery voice.

"Who is there?" Rich asked.

"None of your business young man. We only have business with the three guardians you travel with. Also where do you think you are heading?" Mystery voice said.

"What do you want with us?" Sue asked.

"We are to stop you from finding any more guardians. As well as finding your star princess and prince." Mystery voice said.

"Who are you?" Lola asked.

"We are the generals of the Dark Kingdom Zodiac." Mystery voice.

"What are your names?" Joey asked.

"We are the Gemini twins our powers range from control over the dark earth and dark winds. Our names are Pearl and Jem." The Gemini Twins said together.

"Dark Wind I call you to me." Pearl called.

"Dark Earth I call you to me." Jem called.

"Dark Tornado." Pearl and Jem called together.

"We need to move quickly." Joey yelled.

"Is there any way to stop them?" Lola asked.

"As it stands, no and yes but the thing is you two won't be any help with this fight because of your powers would add to their power over this dark tornado. I can summon a dragon but not sure which one yet." Joey said.

"We need to figure something out before they kill us and destroy this beautiful forest." Sue yelled over the howling of the wind.

"Then let us find some type of shelter." Rich yelled.

"No, we need to stand and fight." Lola yelled back.

Chapter 7

✴

"What do you think we should do if your powers are no good against them?" Rich asked

"I'm not sure what we should do but we need to come up with an idea on how to beat them at their own game." Lola yelled.

"I have an idea." Sue yelled.

"What is it?" Joey, Rich, and Lola yelled back to her.

"Joey summons your ice dragon to freeze the tornado which would stop the wind and earth coming together." Sue yelled at Joey.

"Good idea cuz." Joey yelled.

"I summon the Ice Dragon to me." Joey yelled.

The Ice Dragon appeared and as they are fighting the Gemini Twins, he has his dragon freeze the tornado which did stop the wind and earth coming together. While they had time the four rans as far as they could before night fell upon them away from the twins to get a better chance of winning the next round because they knew that the twins would not stop looking for them until they are stopped, or the guardians can find the Wind Guardian. So, the four started to set up camp for the night hoping for a little sleep, but there would have to be shifts to watch out for the twins and any other problems that might come their way. The only thing was to see who would take first watch.

"I will take for watch because Rich has no type of powers to help protect from the Dark Kingdom Zodiac." Sue said.

"I will sit with you, that way we have better chance of keeping watch and I don't think it is a really good idea for us women to sit in the dark by our self's." Lola said.

"I agree with you, and then I will take second watch in a few hours." Joey said.

"I will take the last watch whether or not I have powers I know this forest better than any of you." Rich said.

"Okay you are good when it comes to knowing the forest, but if the Gemini Twins attacks you have no chance against them." Lola said.

"I may not have much of a chance, but I am not a coward that runs from an enemy like that. Even if it cost me my life, I will protect those who mean the world to me." Rich said.

"Okay, then you can take the last watch, but if they come you better get us so that we can help." Sue said.

Rich and Joey went into the tent to get some rest but could not fall asleep right away because of all the events of the day. Sue and Lola were outside watching for the enemy, and they were talking.

"Sue tells me some things about Joey?" Lola asked.

"What do you want to know?" Sue answered.

"What is his favorite color, what does him like, what kind of sports does he enjoy? Things like that." Lola said.

"Well, you should know that I don't know much about Joey, the reason is his family moved away when we were young, and this is the first time we have seen each longer than five minutes online. It is also the first time we have seen each other in person in like 10 years. The only thing that I know is he likes football and basketball, and his favorite color is red." Sue said.

"Oh. I was just wondering. Sorry, that you did not get to grow up together and become close." Lola said.

"It is okay, we both would have gone our own ways someday. Look shooting stars." Sue said.

As the girls kept watch; they were watching the stars fly across the night sky while the guy's sleep. It was a clear night sky as dark as midnight blue. It was so peaceful that they knew would not last much longer with the Dark Zodiac causing pain, and suffering were ever they go and touch. Finally, when the time had gone by the Joey came out to relieve the girls so that they could get some sleep before they head out at first light. Joey was on watch and when he looked up, he saw that there were stars falling across the sky. He made a wish on the shooting stars and hoped that one day it will come true. A few hours later out walk Rich ready to relieve Joey from watch.

"Hey man, I will get you guys up once I see the dawn lights. Okay." Rich said.

"Sounds like a plan to me." Joey replied.

Rich was keeping watch at the entrance to the camp until it was time to get the others up. Out the corner of his eye he saw something move among the trees. He gets his weapon ready just in case it attacked. As he is watching he sees something else move on his left side and before he knew it, they were surround by giant Ants trying to eat them while they sleep.

"EVERYONE GET UP WE ARE UNDER ATACK!!!!" Rich yelled into the tent.

The first to come running out was Joey because he was the only one other than Rich still awakes because he could not get back to sleep. As he runs out, he damn near runs into one of the giant Ants.

"HOLY SHIT!!!! Where did they come from?" Joey yelled.

"We must be close to the temple because that is near where they live in their Ant hill." Rich yelled back.

"What is going on out here?" Lola and Sue asked together.

As they came running out to join the others they look up and see.

"WHAT THE FUCK." Lola yelled.

"WHAT ARE THEY?" Sue yelled.

"They are giant Ants." Lola answered.

"Yeah, what gave you that clue?" Joey said.

"Don't be a smart ass, okay." Lola said.

"Be careful everyone they spit fire as well." Rich yelled.

"Then in that case we need something that will corner their attack." Joey said.

"Yeah, we also need room to be able to move. Let us head to the river which is only a few feet away." Rich yelled.

"Lead the way to the river." Sue yelled.

All three guardians' followed Rich to the Chesapeake River were they can make a stand against the giant ants that was following them because they were food. As the guardians' try to keep Rich safe as well as defend themselves; it was not easy. Joey had to use his powers of summoning to call fourth his Water Dragon to keep the ants at bay. As they are defending against the giant ants which is pushing them to the edge of the mountain the river was under them and so the Giant Ants had pushed so hard, they fell into the river, Joey was still controlling the Water Dragon he had summon then lost control as they fell into the river. The Water Dragon had disappeared when he hit the water with the rest of the group. They managed to survive the fall only because Sue had made a light portal in the middle of the fall to transport them close to the river without losing their lives. Joey had carried Lola out of the river because she is out cold with the hit from the river and being the Fire Guardian; water was not her best friend. So, the four friends had come out of the river alive and were walking for a little while, while Joey had carried Lola a very good distance in the Jade Forest. As they are still walking, they notice that Rich had stopped.

"What is up man?" Joey asked.

"We need to be very careful in this area of the forest it is a lot more dangerous than the area we were just in. Also, we need to set up camp here because Lola needs rest, and the rest of us need to eat and get dried off." Rich said.

"Do we still have food left after that fall?" Sue asked.

"No; I lost my backpack back there, and thanks for saving our necks." Rich said.

"Yeah; Sue that was quick thinking on your part." Joey said.

"Thanks guys, but we need to find some food." Sue said.

"Leave it to me. I will get us some food, and you two can start setting up the camp while I get us some food." Rich said.

"Okay, just one question. How far are we from the Temple of Emerald?" Sue asked.

"Our walk that should have only taken two days; has now turned into like a week depending on if we keep being attacked by the monsters of this forest and I am guessing the Dark Kingdom Zodiac is behind the attacks. Also, if we run into those Gemini Twins again then we can say we will be here for a while. Right now, just rest and keep watch, and finish setting up camp. I am going to get us some food, and I think Lola might be out for a little while as well." Rich said.

"Okay." Sue agreed.

Rich had left the three guardians to go get food and was going to search the area to find a better or quicker way to the temple. As Joey and Sue set up camp, Joey laid Lola down so he could lend a hand to Sue. As the two guardians took watch, they were looking at the area they were in. It had a lot of trees, flowers, very hot and humid, and as they kept watch things seemed to be getting darker as well. In this part of the Jade Forest, it was very dark; very little sun came though the thickness of the trees. Some would say it was like the trees were giving shelter from rain, and sun. It also provided shade to help keep a little cool. But there was something about the air that unsettled the guardians to no end. The heirs on the back of their necks were standing up as if someone was watching them from a very far place.

"Joey, something doesn't seem right." Sue said.

"I know what you mean. Do you think we can trust Richard?" Joey asked.

"Well, next time save the family talk for more peaceful times. I have some food it may not be what you are used to, but it will give us strength to keep going. I think we should stay here for the night. I will take first watch, but Joey if able can you summon a Fire Dragon to make us a fire. These trees are thick enough that no monster or Dark Kingdom Zodiac can see the smoke." Rich said.

"Yeah. I summon you Fire Dragon." Joey called.

The Fire Dragon had appeared and as always, he looks at Joey thinking why you summoned me again. Joey had asked the Fire Dragon to start the fire so they could eat. Rich had picked some mangos, pears, pineapples, apples, bananas, and coconuts. He had picked enough to get them through the night and morning and for a few days supple. He had made a basket out of banana leaves to put the supple in. Also, he had hunted a few rabbits for them to eat for the night. So, all three friends had started to eat some of the fruit while the rabbits cooked. Rich wanted to tell a story about a kingdom that was growing and destroyed after many years.

"Rich thanks for getting us some food." Sue said.

"You are very welcome. Would you guys like to hear a story about a kingdom that had been growing for many years?" Rich asked.

"Sure, is it about the Majestic Star Kingdom? The Wind Kingdom? OR is it about a kingdom out of a fantasy book?" Sue asked.

"I would have to say it is about the Majestic Star Kingdom from what I was told growing up." Rich said.

"Then please due tell us what you have heard." Joey said.

"The Majestic Star Kingdom; lived a very kind and gentle ruler; he was so in love with a woman from a different realm that he wanted her by his side as he ruled over the kingdom he inherited from his parents. The kingdom was so beautiful that it had a Crystal Castle that could be seen miles away. The woman felt that she was not good enough for the kind ruler as she was not of royal blood. This did not matter to the kind ruler, because he was in love with her. So, the woman agreed to marry the kind ruler and they were very happy for a long time, but one day she wanted a child that will inherit the kingdom and be the kindest, most powerful ruler of the Majestic Star Kingdom that if there was an heir to the throne then there could be peace made between the Majestic Star Kingdom and the Elemental Realm, but for there to be peace the Majestic Star Kingdom would have to bare a baby girl. It took a long time for the Queen to become pageant with the child and in so months later a baby girl was born that was so beautiful here her was as dark as a raven's feather, eyes that look liked honey. So, the marriage between the peace of the Elemental Realm and the Majestic Star Kingdom was arranged, but what was unexpected was that the princess and prince had fallen madly in love with each other, till one the peace was shattered because of a darkness that approach the Elemental Realm and was taken over by this darkness making the Majestic Star Kingdom to call off the wedding between the princess and prince because they could not be trusted. But the princess was so in love that she would take trips to the Elemental Realm to see the prince and the prince would take trips to the Majestic Star Kingdom to see the princess. The Queen and King knew that the prince of the Elemental Realm could be trusted and asked if he would give his life for the kingdom and the princess. The prince said that he would sacrifice his life to protect her and the kingdom. Then one day the darkness came to the Majestic Star Kingdom and had destroyed it; the same the Dark Prince had claimed that the heir to the Majestic Star Kingdom would be his with her beauty, and he would rule the kingdom, but the prince would not let his true love fall into their hands. So, the Dark Kingdom Zodiac attacked the most beautiful kingdom of all the realms and destroyed it, the prince of the Elemental realm had come to defend the Majestic Star Kingdom from the Dark Kingdom Zodiac and in doing so he was taken by the dark kingdom, at the same time trying to protect the princess. She had thrown herself into the fight using her powers of Water and Ice to protect the prince; and the Dark Queen refused to let them live together, so she had sent her dark powers at them causing them to lose their lives. The Queen and King of the Majestic Star Kingdom had used their powers

"Well first we have found five guardians'; we are looking for the sixth one here in your realm, and second the prince of the Elemental Realm is one of the guardians' that we have found. His name is Leroy Addams, the star princess is who we still need to find." Sue said.

"I see." Rich said.

to save the princess and the prince by sending them a thousand years into the future hoping for peace, and if there came a time that the 12 guardians would be needed, they could be awakened to protect the princess and the prince. But the Queen and King had lost their lives saving those of the 12 guardians', princess, and the prince by using up the last of their powers to send them a thousand years into the future." Rich had finished.

Sue was looking at the fire and tears were falling from her eyes. The story was sad and that the only thing they knew was that the Dark Kingdom Zodiac had return to keep the Majestic Star kingdom from rising again. Also, that there have been five guardians found already. The prince was Leroy Addams of the Crystal Star of the Elemental Realm and that his kingdom had survived this tragedy. He is also one of the guardians. Joey seemed to be off in space with a sad look on his face wondering why this had happened, why they all can't live in peace today.

"Guys I know this is hard for you to hear, but that is the story that has been passed down in my family for years. The Wind Realm as you call my home was one of those great Crystal Star Realms that helped the Majestic Star Kingdom. The fight must go on for all the realms to have peace once again." Rich said

"Rich can I tell you something that you must keep to yourself." Sue asked.

"Sure, what is it?" Rich said.

to save the princess and the prince by sending them a thousand years into the future hoping for peace, and if there came a time that the 12 guardians would be needed, they could be awakened to protect the princess and the prince. But the Queen and King had lost their lives saving those of the 12 guardians', princess, and the prince by using up the last of their powers to send them a thousand years into the future." Rich had finished.

Sue was looking at the fire and tears were falling from her eyes. The story was sad and that the only thing they knew was that the Dark Kingdom Zodiac had return to keep the Majestic Star kingdom from rising again. Also, that there have been five guardians found already. The prince was Leroy Addams of the Crystal Star of the Elemental Realm and that his kingdom had survived this tragedy. He is also one of the guardians. Joey seemed to be off in space with a sad look on his face wondering why this had happened, why they all can't live in peace today.

"Guys I know this is hard for you to hear, but that is the story that has been passed down in my family for years. The Wind Realm as you call my home was one of those great Crystal Star Realms that helped the Majestic Star Kingdom. The fight must go on for all the realms to have peace once again." Rich said.

"Rich can I tell you something that you must keep to yourself." Sue asked.

"Sure, what is it?" Rich said.

"Well first we have found five guardians'; we are looking for the sixth one here in your realm, and second the prince of the Elemental Realm is one of the guardians' that we have found. His name is Leroy Addams, the star princess is who we still need to find." Sue said.

"I see." Rich said.

Chapter 8

As Rich sat there, he could not believe that the prince of the Elemental Realm was alive. He wanted to meet him, and it would be nice to see the princess as well Rich was thinking. Joey had listened to the story Rich had told and could not stop thinking about Leroy and Alena. Something seemed to come to him then he would lose it again as if he was trying to figure out a puzzle. If the princess could be awakened, then peace would come to all the realms, and everyone would be happy. Lola was still out cold from the fall off the cliff early that day when it came time for the friends to get rest Rich had taken first watch and Joey would take second watch living Sue and Lola to rest up. The temple was almost a four day walk now from where they are at. Rich sat in the middle of the night trying to remember what his father had told him about the guardian that would protect their realm and release it from the evil that had taken over. As he thought about it; it was hard to remember because he was so young then that not much about protecting the realm was not that important until he had lost his parents and he was alone then he started to think about how the guardian could do or even look like. He knew that to save his home they had to find this so-called guardian to save the Crystal Star of the Wind Realm. What would happen if they found the guardian would the person be willing to help them, or would they just turn their nose away and walk away from it all? As it got close to wake joey for second watch Rich was still wondering about how there could be guardians in different realms and that those realms really do exist. Joey came out of the tent after resting for a little while to release Rich from his watch. He saw that Rich was off in space wondering about something, he just didn't know what.

"Hey man, get some rest and I will take over watch." Joey said.

As Joey had spoken Rich jumped up pulling out his to daggers and then notice it was Joey standing saying something.

"Oh, hold on man it is just me. I didn't mean to scare you when I said something, sorry." Joey said.

"It is my fault I should have been paying more attention instead of letting my mind wonder." Rich said.

"What were you thinking about?" Joey asked.

"I was thinking about the wind guardian and wondering if they would help us. Also, I was thinking about my father and trying to remember what he told me about the guardian so long ago." Rich said.

"Oh, I see. You know that a guardian can be good or bad depending on what their life was like, and how they grew up. When we find the Wind Guardian then maybe we could get rid of those Gemini Twins for go. Also, that would make one less guardian we have to find so that peace can come to all the realms." Joey said.

"Thanks man that does make me feel a whole lot better." Rich said.

"Why don't you get some rest, and I will finish the watch. When dawn comes, we will wake the girls and keep going on to the temple." Joey said.

"Okay, I live everything to you then." Rich said.

As Rich went into the camp Joey stared after him for a while and then took his position to keep watch. He was wondering if the guardian could be Rich, but he has not showed any signs of having any powers of a guardian, but his heart was as pure as the wind. As Joey sat keeping watch, he notices that things seem to get worse than better they had to make it to the temple and hoping that Lola will come to in the morning he heard a noise coming from behind him and out walked Lola wide awake.

"Hey, how long have I been out cold dude?" Lola said with a laugh.

"You have been out all day and most of the night." Joey answered.

"Oh, wow! That long huh. So, what has happened since I have been out?" Lola asked.

"Well, we are further away from the temple than what we were when we started this trip, and we all fell off the cliff, Sue had used her powers to make a quick portal to get us closer to the water so we would not die, and when we hit the water, you had passed out. Rich had gone ahead and searched the area to see where we are at, and to find out we are now three days away from the temple now." Joey said.

"Oh, is that all. Would you like some company to help keep watch?" Lola said.

"That sounds great to me. We can talk for a minute while the others sleep." Joey said.

"Okay." Lola said.

"Lola, I should tell you that I was in a relationship before we came to your realm. The girl that I'm talking about is another guardian; well, she and I broke up and had a big fight before coming here even though she pretended that there was nothing wrong. Just to let you know she is the guardian of the Crystal Star of Water and Ice. It is over between me and her, but we are still really good friends." Joey told Lola.

"So, what you are saying is when I meet this other guardian not to look too much into it." Lola said.

As the two sat talking until dawn they got the others up and they started walking to the temple hoping that they can avoid fights with the enemy again. As the group is walking it starts to get hotter than before.

"What is going on with this heat?" Sue asked.

"As we get closer to the temple it will get hotter. Just to let you know this is a way to keep travelers away from the temple." Rich said.

"How can we keep from getting burned up if we want to a porch the temple?" Sue asked.

"Well, we can use the river to get to the temple it would keep us cool, and it would shorten our trip." Rich said.

"How are we supposed to use the river if we don't have a boat to use?" Joey asked.

"Well, we could borrow one from the next village or make a raft." Rich said.

"We don't have time to make a raft; we are running out of time. Let us see if there is a boat we could use." Lola said.

"Then I guess we walk a few more miles to get to the next village." Rich said.

"What is the name of the village you want to take us to?" Sue asked.

"It is named after a great hero. The village is called Williamsburg." Rich said.

So, they walk to the village to find that there is no one in site as if the village was like a ghost town. So, they walk down to the docks to see that there was only one boat left that could be used because the other boats had been destroyed. The boat was big enough for the group to use. As the group gets in the boat, they start to row down the river which would cut down the time by almost three quarters. As they sail down the river hoping it would be a smooth ride, but something had hit the bottom of the boat almost tipping it over. When the group of friends stood up to get a better look of what hit them a huge turtle jumped out of the water and spared them with acid water. So, Lola jumped back almost falling into the river.

"Fire come to me." Lola yelled.

"Way to go Lola!" Joey said.

"Good use of your power." Sue said.

"Thank you so much for sending that turtle to the darkness for which it came from." Rich said.

As the fire hit the water turtle it went poof like a water bubble. As it had turned to dust when the fire hit it, they had smooth sailing for the rest of the day. As they got closer to the temple, they went onto the beach that was close to the temple at least a half day left to go when they will reach the temple. As the group sailed onto the beach, they set up camp near the river so that they could keep an eye on the boat. The first to take watch was Sue she would keep an eye on the river and the boat. As Sue is sitting for watch she starts to think about what will happen if they could not find the Wind Guardian to help find the star princess with everything going on she just noticed that they have missed many weeks of school and her GPA is going to the fishes. But as she sat there, she was thinking that it was good that her GPA is not so great even before they went on this journey to find the Star Princess and all the other guardians, but most of all she missed her best friend and all the fun they have together. Also, she was with Prince Leroy of the Crystal Star of the Elemental Realm. She was hoping that they would be getting a long without her being the referee between the two friends. Also thinking of Leroy, they had left things undone between them when Leroy had caught her kissing, Andrew. The she started to think about how handsome he was, how he can kiss which made the world stand still, and most of all his kindness was the best of all. Andrew had the strongest hands that could hold up the earth and keep it from touching the ground for any reason which would make him the best guy to keep her safe. When it was getting late Lola came out to sit with her for a little while until it was time for her to take over the watch while the guys sleep for a little while, because they wanted to get moving soon before dawn so they could make it to the temple and start looking for the Wind Guardian.

"So would you like some company?" Lola asked.

"Yeah, that would be great. Also, it would be great to have someone to talk to." Sue said.

"What have you been thinking about?" Lola asked.

"I was thinking about my other friends back home and what they are doing." Sue said.

"It sounds like you have been second guessing this whole guardian thing or the journey you are on with your cousin." Lola said.

"No, I am not second guessing about being a guardian, because my best friend is also a guardian of the Crystal Star of Water and Ice. She is just not getting along with the Prince of the Crystal Star of the Elemental Realm." Sue said.

"It sounds like you are home sick." Lola said.

"Yeah, most likely that is what it is." Sue said.

"I know how you are feeling because I feel the same way being so far away from my own home. But Joey and you make it a lot better because you gave me something worth fighting for." Lola said.

"Thanks, and I am glad that we could give that to you, and I think I have another best friend to add to my list of friends. Alena and you are like sisters to me. Thanks for that." Sue said.

"Glad that I can do that for you. Now go get some rest and I would take over the watch until it is time to go." Lola said.

As Sue went to bed Lola was smiling from ear to ear, she found friends that was worth fighting for and now that she has them, she will do anything to protect them. She also wanted to meet Alena and hoping that Alena and she can become good friends like Sue and her. Also, she wanted more than anything to meet Alena because Sue has talked about her being a good person and hoping that she will like her for her. As Lola sat there, she had high hopes that Sue, Alena, and her will be good friends. As Lola sets there on her watch, she noticed that the temple could be seen even in the night. This met that they were closer than they thought.

"EVERYONE PLEASE WAKE UP!" Lola yelled.

"What is it?" Rich asked.

"The temple it is close, and I mean very close because you can see in the darkness from the tent, come see." Lola said.

As the other three follow her outside they look where she was pointing and notice that the temple was indeed close.

"Rich how far do you think the temple might be from here?" Lola and Sue asked together.

"Maybe a few hours walk if we get started and no problems from the Dark Kingdom Zodiac." Rich answered.

As the friends gather their things up and move out toward the temple; the forest seemed to be against them as they kept walking it seemed to go up hill and then downhill it was as if the forest was moving. So, the four had stopped for lunch near a Fur Tree that had ripped Star Fruit which was go and juicy when the four friends bet into the Star Fruit it was very sweet. It was yellow, with a soft center.

Chapter 9

The friends worked their way to the temple so they could find a way to help Rich with the Dark Kingdom Zodiac and hopefully find the Wind Guardian. As the group made their way to the temple there was a blockage from a huge Black Widow Spider protecting the entrance to the Emerald Temple in the Forest of Jade.

"Watch out for the spider's web it has acid its in." Rich said. As the Black widow had spit its spider web at the group.

"Where did that huge thing come from. I HATE SPIDERS!" Sue yelled.

"Well in this case I think we can get rid of it." Joey said.

As the four friends had pulled out their weapons they had to jump out of the way when another spider had come out of the temple and spit its web at the group.

"How do you like our pets?" Gemini Twins said together.

"The Dark Kingdom Zodiac strikes again." Rich yelled.

"Oh, we have been tracking you four a while now. When you fell off the cliff and the Giant Ants attacked all of you. Not only that we want to thank you for leading us here." Gemini Twin Pearl said.

"How dare you use us to get what you wanted. So, what was that?" Lola asked.

"Oh, it is just that we want to keep the next guardian from being found which would make it harder for you to find the others." Gemini Twin Jem said.

"The Dark Kingdom needed something from us, well I got news for you we don't know who the Wind Guardian is." Sue said.

"Are you sure you have not found that guardian yet." Pearl said.

"Yell, we are pretty sure we have not found the guardian yet. Rich is not a guardian but has a heart of one because he is brave, strong, and cares about his people which you took from him." Joey said.

"I am not a guardian of this realm. Thanks Joey." Rich said.

"From what I can see you have dormient powers of wind. You think because you don't have the powers of wind that you could not be a guardian. Then we know something you don't. If you can bet our pets, then we will let you pass and see what is at the end of temple." The Gemini Twins said.

"Well, it looks like we might be kind of busy. So, it might take us a little longer to get to the back of the temple." Rich said.

"Well then I think we need to get busy." Joey said.

"I summon the Fire Dragon." Joey called.

"Fire Rings come to me." Lola called.

"Light Balls come to me." Sue called.

"I might not have powers, but I can fight hand to hand combat." Rich said.

"Then show us what you got." Gemini Twins said together.

As the four friends fight the Giant Black Widows in front of the Gemini Twins just to come out on top by getting though the door before they could finish off the Giant Black Widows. So, the friends started down the temple to find many doorways for them to pick from. Also, to found traps in each doorway and tunnels in many directions. It would be that if they spilt up it could bad. As the friends try and choose which tunnel would be best, they seemed to think that they can't agree with each other.

"I think that we should take the tunnel on the far left." Lola said.

"I think that we should take the center tunnel to the right." Sue said.

"Rich, who one does you think would be best?" Joey asked.

"To be honest I'm not sure which way we should go because I have never been in this part of the temple before." Rich replied.

"Then the majority vote which tunnel we should take will be the tunnel we go down." Joey said.

"In favor of going down the tunnel on the far right rise your hand." Rich said.

As the four agree to take the center tunnel to the left just to be blocked by a huge falcon. As the friends start to go near the bird just to be almost eaten by the huge bird. This met that there was something in that tunnel worth protecting. So, they tried to a pouch the huge falcon again only to jump back to keep from getting eaten. As the friends try to figure out how to get pass the bird to get down the tunnel just to hear something a pouch from behind as they turned around, they seen some from Jurassic period and even bigger than the falcon that was blocking their way through. Now they were blocked from both sides just to be forced to use their powers yet again even though they were tired from fighting against the Giant Black Widows. As they fight the dinosaur that was trying to eat them just to be pushed back near the falcon which again tried to grab them with its beak because it thought they are food to eat. Just to be pushed back near the dinosaur again just to have the dinosaur's teeth that was about 10 inches long and very pointy which worriers from old still stuck in its month.

"Oh, did we tell you that we have pets all over the temple to keep you guardians out." Gemini Twins appeared and said.

"The Black Widows were a trap just to trick us into coming into the temple just to be caught between a rock and a hard place." Lola said.

"Oh, don't say it like that. All we wanted to do was have fun with you and what we have heard that you are strong in your powers. So, we wanted to see how you would do with our pets and no way out." Gemini Twin Pearl said.

"Then how would you like me to say it then. There is no reason to be nice to you; all you have done was giving us hell this whole time we have been here not only that all the Dark Kingdom Zodiac does wreak havoc on the realms." Lola said.

"So, you think that you have what it takes to bet us and our pets?" Jem said.

"DAMN RIGHT WE DO!!!!" Sue yelled.

"Light come to me!" Sue called.

"Fire comes to me." Lola said.

"I summon the water dragon." Joey said.

As the three guardians release their powers into the dinosaur and the falcon to open the tunnel a head the Gemini Twins was very angry about the guardians getting away for a third time. As they run down the tunnel to get away, they needed to find the sixth guardian of the Crystal Star Realm of Wind. The Wind guardian would be their only hope. As they enter a room that was so big, they could not take it all in. Then in the middle of the room was a glow of green and gold. As they started to a pouch a gust of wind came up and surrounds them to keep them from getting near the golden and green glow. Rich could somehow stand the power of the wind when the others had fell to their knees trying to keep from passing out. Somehow, they needed to get to that glow in the middle of the room to get the wind to stop. Then Rich got this strange feeling as if someone was talking to him in his mind.

"Trust in yourself and your friends. Become a better Wind Guardian than me, my son. You are the rightful heir to the throne of the Crystal Star of the Wind Realm. We served the Majestic Star Kingdom long ago and we had failed in that, so we have shunned away from the other realms only in the end to destroy ourselves. Try to understand my son that we made a huge mistake because we felt that we would never be good enough to protect the Star Princess or her prince, so I hid the powers of the Wind Guardian in that crown that has green leaves, and vines that go into a circle. Put the crown on and claim your true power, and if you can forgive me, my son for my mistakes in the past and not trusting you to become the man you are today." Rich's father said.

The other guardians heard the voice in their heads as well and turned toward the floating crown to see a ghost of the man that looked so much like Rich that there was no mistake this was the last guardian only to be given the next guardian of the Crystal Star of the Wind Realm. Also, on top of that it had to be Rich's father. As the guardians looked on, they saw that Rich could stand in the Wind that was surrounding them and that he was able to walk out of the wind tunnel and started to walk toward the ghost.

"How do I know that I am worthy of the powers? How sure are you that I can do this?" Rich asked his father.

"I know because you made friends with these other guardians who have changed you this past month. Not only that they believe in you more than I did. Your heart is as pure as the wind. All you must do is touch the crown and my powers and blood line run though you. They will become yours as it was supposed to be." Rich's father said.

As Rich walked to his father only to hesitate to touch the crown because he was still unsure about his own self; more than those that are around him. When he reached out to touch the crown when the Gemini Twins appeared in the room with their Giant Black Widows. So, before Rich could grab the crown he went flying across the room and hitting the wall on the far left. As the Gemini Twins tried to grab the crown, they felt a hot heat and in turn burning their hands after touching the crown of the Wind Realm. So instead of grabbing the crown the Black Widows spit their acid spider web at the crown, tangling it up in the web. Even the acid web could not hurt the crown because it was protected by a power that was not seen.

"You cannot touch the crown of the Wind Realm it is protected by the mystery power of good and the Majestic Star Kingdom." Luke said.

"If we can't have the crown of the wind realm or the wind guardian's powers then you will not have a guardian at all." Pearl said.

"Dark Wind come to me." Pearl called.

"Dark Wind Blade come to me." Jem said.

As the two generals of the Dark Kingdom Zodiac aimed their powers near Rich the wind tunnel seemed to stop and when it did stop the other guardians went to help him.

"Fire I call you to me to help protect Rich." Lola called.

"Light I call you to me please make a shield around Rich." Sue called.

"I summon the Ice Dragon to me." Joey called.

As the shield went around Rich it was just in a nick of time. But just to see the powers shot back at the Gemini Twins missing them by inches. As the guardians keep fighting for their friend and their future and while they were fighting Rich came to. Watching in wide eyed his friends fighting for him and his realm. Before Rich could think he ran from the shield and grabbed the Wind Crown. When he touched the crown this warm breeze that smelled of summer and spring together. He felt this warm heat in his hands, but he was not being burned just the opposite he felt full of love, kindness, and most of all he felt that he could do more than just stood by and watched his friends become fish food.

"I beg of you Wind please bend to my will and help to protect my friends from the Gemini Twins generals of the Dark Kingdom Zodiac has returned and is tiring to take away our freedom again." Rich pleaded.

As the guardians was surround by a wind tunnel again, but it was different than last time because this had the feeling of love in it and strength that could be felt all over the Wind Realm. Then the guardians look and see Rich standing and holding the crown of the Wind Realm, and they knew they had found the sixth guardian of the Crystal Star of the Wind Realm. Then Rich goes near the Gemini Twins and was going to stop them on his own.

"Wind I call you to me. Blow those Gemini Twins to oblivion." Rich called.

As the wind power hit the Gemini Twins, they went poof like a dust cloud. When Rich released the wind tunnel around his friends, he looked at his father and then passed out.

"My son you have done well. You have proved that you are a true Wind Guardian. I leave in your hands to protect the Star Princess and Prince. Also leave you the future of our realm. May you bring peace again to us and make amends with the Majestic Star Kingdom. Stay well my son." Luke said.

As Luke had said to Rich he turned to the other guardians and knelt his head and said "thank you for being his friends. Please show him how to be a true guardian and find the Star Princess, she is the only one that came give us all peace." As he said his last words he disappeared into the beyond where ghost go to have peace. As the friends walked over to Rich, they knew they didn't have much time to get out of the temple as it had started to shake. With the Wind Guardian found the temple was falling apart and the friends were very thankful for his help this whole time and that with the wind powers now to the right person the Temple of Emerald was not needed. So, the friends picked Rich up between them and ran through the door for which they came through the first time. Then back toward the front of the temple just to watch the temple to go up in smoke. Then the temple fell by falling in on the suction.

Chapter 10

As the group had made camp, they needed to make plans to send both Lola and Rich back to the Crystal Star Realm of Water and Ice. Lola did not like the idea of leaving either one of her friends and most of all she did not want to leave Joey. She loved him more than life, but knew she had a job to do. To have peace for her realm she needed to find the Star Princess and the other guardians needed to be found and this was his and Sue's mission to their friends. She would not be going a lone Rich would be with her.

Rich was still out cold from using his powers and she could relate to how tired he might be with everything needed to be processed. The three Guardians made camp a few miles away from the fallen temple and let Rich rest after using his true powers for the first time. As the friends look around to make sure that there were no more enemies in the area. They start to talk about whom take watch, but they will not agree with each, so they all choose to stand watch over the camp site as Rich was sleeping. From first time of using their own powers they knew Rich would be out at least 1-2 days which gives them all time to come up with a plan to get the other guardians back to the Crystal Star of Water and Ice Realm. Sue would have to make two portals one for them to get back and one for them to move forward, but first they need to get to the castle to find some information on the other guardians, but to do this they needed Rich and him up to bat. So, as they talk the guardians started to argue, Lola didn't want to leave their side, and this made both Joey and Sue feel great but they knew they need to go to the Crystal Star of Water and Ice Realm and help their friends to find the Star Princess just so they can have peace.

"I don't want to leave you both." Lola said.

"We understand but we all have our own mission and right now this is Joey's and mine. Rich and you need to help our friends to find the Star Princess so that we all can have peace." Sue said.

"I have to agree with Sue, but I don't want to leave you either Lola, but Sue is right you have a mission, and we do." Joey said.

"I know that, but I don't want to leave either of you. I know we will have to." Lola said.

"I don't want either of you to leave, but it is what it is." Joey said.

"Look at it this way when we have found all the guardians and then we will return to the Crystal

Star of Water and Ice, and you two can be together. Not only that we all will be together and start looking for the Star Princess. Okay." Sue said.

"Okay, it doesn't make it any easier, but durable." Lola said.

"I agree." Joey said.

They had talked through the night, and they saw the sun on the horizon, and they saw a new future in the works. There were friends around every corner and new thing to discover, but right now they needed to get to that castle in the distance. They needed to get to that castle to get much needed information about other guardians. Also, they needed to find some food, or they would not last much longer and using their powers will just drain them of what energy they have left. So, each one took turns looking for food and keeping an eye on Rich while he rests and gets his energy back but would not work unless he gets some food and water in him soon. So as the guardians took turns to find food, water, and making plans to get to the castle and fast. Rich started to wake up, as his eyes fluttered and then started to open, he saw that it was night and his friends where at the entrance to the tent talking, and from what he got from their conversation it was about him and other guardians. He started to get up and lay back down because he became dizzy and was very weak from his fight. Then he started to remember what happened at the temple and how he saw his father. Then learned that his father was once the wind guardian, but now he is. Could he, do it? Will he make a good guardian? Could he help the others find the Star Princess so that there will one day be peace in all the realms. All of this was running though his mind as Sue walked in and saw him a wake, she bent down next to him on the ground to make sure he was okay.

"How are you feeling?" Sue asked.

"Sore, tired, and a lot of confusion." Rich said.

"Well, I know that feeling all too well." Sue said.

"What do you mean?" Rich asked.

"Let me tell you something about guardians, and me. Will you lay there and listen?" Sue asked.

"Yes, please tell me about them." Rich said.

"Okay, he goes nothing. It started back on the Crystal Star Realm of Water and Ice. There were things going on I didn't know about or really didn't take the time to find out. One of my best friends is the Guardian of Water and Ice Crystal Star Realm; another is a Guardian of the Element Crystal Star Realm. The Dark Kingdom Zodiac was attacking, and Alena had to take the Dark Kingdom on all by herself and when Joey came along; he helped, there was another guy at the time that helped as well. Just to find out he turned out to be Leroy who he is also the Prince of the Crystal Star of Element Realm. When Alena had been taken by the Dark Kingdom Zodiac, they needed my help and when they told me who I am. I freaked out and ran out on them and when I choose to go with them to the Dark

Kingdom Zodiac Realm to help save Alena and well just as you found out I had found out that there was such a thing as the Dark Kingdom Zodiac and their generals that want to whack havoc on all the realms and rule them. I found out that by protecting those that matter to me most was worth is the Guardian of Light from the Crystal Star Realm of Light and Travel. Now I have better control over my powers and have helped a lot of people out. Now that you know and all, why don't I get you some food and you rest a little while longer. We will be heading to the Wind Castle to free your realm and get more information on the other guardians." Sue said.

"Thanks for telling me. I would like to rest a little while and think about all of this." Rich said.

"Okay, I will go get you some food and water okay." Sue said.

"Okay." Rich said.

As Sue left Rich to rest, she went and told the others that he was awake, and she got him some food and water and took it to him. He was still awake when she walked in the tent. Then turned and looked at her and smiled, he never thought that he would have some good friends and that he was the true heir to the throne of the Wind Realm. He had been thinking and chose to go with them to find and free the Star Princess.

"How are you feeling?" Sue said.

"A lot better now. Thank you." Rich said as he was sitting up to eat.

"Glad to hear that. We will be heading out at first light and Joey is going to summon one of his dragons and fly us to the castle." Sue said.

"I think that we will be able to rich the castle this time without any more problems from the Dark Kingdom Zodiac since we got rid of their generals." Rich said.

"Well said. Now rest and I will wake you up as soon as it is time to leave. Okay." Sue said.

"Okay. Will you be resting as well?" Rich asked.

"Yeah, I will be resting first, Lola and Joey are going to keep watch and then wake me in a few hours, and I will wake everyone up when it is time." Sue said.

"Okay." Rich said.

As Rich fell back to sleep, he dreamed of a castle out of a fantasy book. The castle was made up of Crystals of all colors and it shined so bright that it was hard to miss, but something about the castle seemed to be welcoming and warm. It was full of life, there was music in the distances, and he was sitting in the field of flowers that looked as it could be rich to the ends of the world. As he got up, he was wearing a tuxedo of Jade Green with orange crystals. He was dress up for a party and a very beautiful woman reached her hand out to him and he took it. It was as if he knew who she was she was in the most beautiful grown of orange with jade green crystals all over it. As they entered the ballroom everyone seemed to be standing around looking on to someone dancing in the middle of the ballroom. It was a girl and guy; the girl was so beautiful she had to be the star princess. The guy dancing with her had to be the prince of the Elemental Realm. As Rich was dreaming, he was filled with such warmth that he could be the guardian of the Wind Realm. As Rich was sleeping someone was calling him and shaking him to wake up. As he started to wake, he notices that it was Sue waking him. When she saw that he was a wake she went onto Lola, and the Joey.

"Did you all sleep well?" Sue asked.

"Yes." Joey, Lola, and Rich said together.

"Well shawl we all get going. Joey you can summon the Wind Dragon, right?" Sue asked.

"Yes, I can, and you think we can eat first?" Joey asked.

"I guess you can." Sue said.

The friends started to eat something before getting things together so they can head to the Wind Castle. As they finished eating and got all their things together Joey had summoned his Wind Dragon and they all climbed onto the back of the dragon. As they few though the air to the castle, there seemed to be something off. As they approached there seemed to be a wind cloud around the castle.

"Rich can you control the wind around the castle?" Joey asked.

"Let me try." Rich said.

As Rich tried to control the wind would not bend to his will. It was as if it has dark powers in it.

"I don't think I can, there seems to be something dark about it." Rich said.

"Then we need to figure out how to get past that wind cloud." Lola said.

"Welcome guardians. I'm the Joker and I'm here to stop you from going any further." Joker said.

"What another general from the Dark Kingdom?" Sue asked.

"Well, you are right, but I will not fight you here. I have seen your fight with the Gemini Twins, and you are very strong, but I'm stronger and you have no chance." The Joker said.

"Then what are you going to do?" Sue asked.

"I will let you pass. Get stronger and then face me." The Joker said.

"Then we will, and we will face you when the time comes." Joey said.

As he said this the wind cloud had stopped and the guardians where able to approach the castle and go inside. As they went inside Rich was able to go to the throne room and it was so bear with webs, and dust. As he went in, he sat on the throne, and he made a vow that when this is all over and done with, he can come back here and rule the Wind Realm like he is supposed to. The guardians went through all the rooms and found the library and as they start to look though the books as they did, they learned that there was a mirror that can transport them to any realm they needed to go. The next realm is the Lighting Realm, and the mirror was in the master bedroom of the castle. Before Joey and Sue can go to the Lighting Realm the other two had to go to the Crystal Star of Water and Ice Realm.

"Lola and Rich, I'm sorry about this but we need you to go to the Crystal Star of Water and Ice Realm. We have friends waiting for you and word from us. It is Joey and my mission to find all the other guardians." Sue said.

"Why can't we go with you?" Rich asked.

"The reason is because Sue can't transport all of us at the same time. Maybe three but not four or more, it would drain her to much that she could be out for days to weeks." Joey said.

"We understand." Lola said.

"Thanks. Please tell Alena and Leroy that we are finding, and we are starting to learn more and more about the Majestic Star Kingdom and Star Princess. Also let them know that we are doing well." Sue said.

Sue opened the portal for Rich and Lola to go through to the Crystal Star of Water and Ice Realm. As the two other guardians went through the portal to come out on the other side with a few people waiting for them.

"Welcome to the Crystal Star of Water and Ice. These people right here are my friends. Protector Glen, Guardian of Elemental Realm Leroy Addams, Alena Patches, and I'm Jennifer Muse you can call me Jenny." Jennifer said.

"Hi, my name is Richard Springer, and this is Lola James. You can call me Rich. I am from the Crystal

Star of Wind Realm, and Lola is from the Crystal Star of Fire." Rich said.

"It is nice to meet you both." Alena said.

"Sue and Joey said to tell you they are doing well and are on their way to the Crystal Star of Lighting realm." Lola said.

"Thanks for letting us know. I know it had to be hard for you to leave them and come here." Leroy said.

"Yes, but we know it was our mission to come here, and theirs' to find the remaining guardians. We also have been told who you are your majesty." Rich said.

"They informed you of that and we are looking for the Star Princess. We are also looking for the prince as well. Together both the star princess and prince to rule the new Majestic Star Kingdom." Leroy said.

"Yes." Lola said.

While Joey and Sue watch both Rich and Lola go through the portal. It is time to close this portal and open the portal to the Crystal Star of Lighting Realm. As they walk into the portal, they step out on the other side just to hear and see lightning striking the ground and a nearby statue blowing off the head. Then before they know it lightning strikes 10cm from where they are standing. The lightning is blue, purple, red, and green. These lightning strikes are very different than any other realm they have been. Seen as this lightning can very dangerous and most likely deadly.

"Are you ready for this Sue?" Joey asked.

"As ready as I'm gonna be. But I don't think the odds are in are favor. I would say we have maybe a 20% chance of surviving. What do you think?" Sue asked.

"I think that we could survive about 45%. Wanna bet on it?" Joey asked.

"Sure, why not. What are we betting on then? What is the prize if the person loses?" Sue asked.

"If you lose then you have to cook dinner for the week and have to take first watch when we set up camp. Do you agree?" Joey said.

"Okay, your on. Better take out that stopwatch to see who the winner of this contest will be." Sue said. Joey took out his watch and got ready to set the stopwatch for their race.

The Crystal
Star of the
Lightning Realm

Chapter 11

As they walked out of the portal; they notice that there were lightning rods everywhere. It was dark and there were storm clouds. The rods where attracting the lighting strikes to the rods like every few minutes. As Sue and Joey walked out and they notice many things at once. They saw a tower in the distance, more lightning, some huge lightning rods, and pillars that had lighting rods attached to the pillars. Every time lightning would strike Sue would jump, she hated storms, even more when there was lighting, and thunder involved. So, when lightning hit a rod, she would jump and Joey would start to laugh, but stopped when he saw her face and how scared she was.

"What do you think would happen if we try to cross this field with all that lightning hitting?" Sue asked.

"I'm not sure, but we need to be careful. It might not be pretty if we get fired by lighting for some reason or another. Not only that our best chance to get though this is to aim for the pillars with lightning rods in between lightning strikes to keep from being hit with lightning. So, we need to time the strikes." Joey said.

"Got ya. Here goes nothing." Sue said.

As the two guardians watch on, they were counting the lightning strikes would come every 3-5 seconds. So, they had to run for the first pillar which was about a one city block from where they stand under a tree that had been struck by lightning a while ago. As they count the 3-5 seconds, then ran to the pillar which did not make it much better since it had started to rain, but there was someone else in the lightning field running from one pillar to the next one. She seemed to be very good at it, as if this was some type of sport that the people of this realm did for fun.

"Joey, do you see that person running from pillar to pillar? I notice the person after we got to this pillar." Sue asked.

"Yeah, I see them. They do this a lot or something. Maybe they can help us out by pointing us in the right direction we need to go to find the castle or even a town of this realm and start looking for the lightning guardian of this realm." Joey replied.

"Yeah, hopefully they can help us out. Right now, would be the time to run for the next pillar." Sue said.

As they two ran for the next pillar they notice that there are many trees that seemed to have been hit with lightning. Also, the tower stands by itself which would be a good place to start looking for the next guardian. As the lightning strikes each pillar the two guardians made their way to the last pillar only to see that the end of the field was quite the distance from where the pillar was at. They had run to about 19 pillars only to get discourage on the last one. Sue was counting the pillars as they ran to each one in between lightning strike. She had counted 19 pillars which did not include the one they are at which would make it 20 pillars and the last pillar was further away from the end of the field that it was going to take them a little longer to get out of this field. Sue was getting very anxious to be going because she did not like the lightning and thunder she was hearing, not only that it started to rain heaver which made it hard to see across the field anymore. It also seemed that the rain got heaver with every pillar.

"On my count of three we make a run for the end of the field." Joey said.

"Okay, but why can't you summon a dragon to carry us to the end of the field?" Sue asked.

"The reason is simply, because of the lightning no dragon will come, and we have no idea when we might need our powers with the Dark Kingdom Zodiac, and their general the Joker on the loose." Joey said.

"Good point. Okay on three then. Get that stopwatch ready because I'm about to win this bet." Sue said.

"In your dreams cuz. On 3 we run. Stopwatch started. 1....... 2....... 3 RUNS!" Joey yelled.

The two guardians made it to the end of the field just in a nick of time because as they reached the end of the field the pillar, they had been at got hit with a big lightning strike making the pillar fall to the ground. This was not a good thing for the next person who wants to make the field a go. Then lightning strike just an inch or two from where they are standing. So, Joey and Sue made a run for it down a flight of stairs and right into a group of people standing around listening to someone talk. This person had to be some type of religious folk because he was wearing a robe of violet purple. It would have been a nice robe if the color was different. So, Joey and Sue take a minute to listen and rest only to be pushed back by the other people standing around listening to him speak. It was like this guy was some type of super star that people wanted to get a picture of and wanted to touch. So, Joey had an idea to ask the people who he was.

"Excuse me sir who might the speaker be?" Joey asked.

"You are in my way MOVE." Guy, one said.

"Sorry, but can you please tell me who he might be I'm new here." Joey pleaded.

The guy just kept walking away from him and pushing him out of the way. Joey seemed not to be able to get anywhere with the population. So, he quick trying to ask anyone.

"Let me try okay." Sue said.

"Fine give it a try, you might just get us somewhere." Joey said.

"Excuse me sir can you please help me. I'm kind a lost, and I'm new here." Sue said.

"Sure, young lady. What do you want to know?" Guy two said.

"Who is speaking?" Sue asked.

"The man that is speaking is the master of the church and temple that is the most properly to the royal family which has the gift of controlling the lightning. Something has been off a lot lately, like something or someone is interfering with the lightning." Guy two said.

"What you are saying, he is the head of the church like a priest or monk, and the royal family is the ones who control the lightning going on here." Sue said.

"Yeah, that about sums it up." Guy two said.

After Sue had found out some information for both Joey and her to find the next guardian. In this case they needed to go to the castle to find the royal family and hopeful the next guardian. More people had come to hear the man talk more about respecting the Gods of lightning to get the lightning from going crazy. It had been a long day so the people wanted to rest and listen because they knew that the Gods would fix whatever was wrong.

"What do you think we should do now, there is too many people to get by?" Sue asked.

"We can rest at a pub or saloon and go from there." Joey said.

"Okay, let us find a place to rest." Sue said.

As the two-start walking down the road to find a place to rest; they notice the same person that was running through the lightning field they had just came out of. Only to find out; up close by walking by; she was a girl with violet hair and amber eye color. It was odd to see a person with these features, she seemed to be out of place as if this spokesperson was full of himself and just playing the people for fools. She seemed to have a discussed looked on her face like he was lying or just pretending that he believes what he was saying. Sue and Joey kept walking and pretended they did not notice her, as they kept walking then notice a hotel and walked in. As they approached the front desk.

"Excuse me; are there any rooms that are open for renting?" Sue asked.

"Hello, how can I help you? We have a couple of rooms left, but all rooms have one bed for couples honeymooning. There are a few double beds available as well." Secretary said.

"We will take one room with two beds for my wife and me just got married and am looking for a good honeymoon." Joey said.

"Okay, for one room with two beds that would be $150 a night." Secretary said.

"Okay we will take the room for five days." Joey said.

"That will be $750." Secretary said.

"Here uses my visa card to pay for the room and anything that my beautiful new wife might want." Joey said.

The security had charged Joey's credit card for the room and whatever they might need for the next five days to look for the next guardian.

"Room 315. Congratulation on your marriage." Sectary said.

"Thank you very much." Sue said.

"Welcome and enjoy your stay." Sectary said.

As both took the elevator to their room on the 300th floor they seen a lot of unique things like the elevator was made of glass and floor so you could look all over the land of the Lightning Realm. They notice that the flowers where like crystals shinning in the partly cloudy sky now. It looks almost like mist was coming from the flowers because they changed all kinds of shade of purple. The realm was different from the other realms they have been to recently. Each realm is unique to that realm. There was a nice breeze outside of the elevator the only reason they knew this because the trees where swaying in the breeze which was also different because the tree leaves looked dark purple on top and light purple on the bottom. Joey had looked up at the sky and noticed that the sky was like a very light purple even though it was only maybe midday here. It was very beautiful in its own way, but also unique as well. Once the elevator reached the 300th floor they got off and took a right to their room and to discover that it had a huge king size bed, with purple silk sheets, lavender comforter, with big pillows that also had some shade of purple on the pillowcases. The bed was inviting them to sleep because they had been very tired from their trip to the Lightning Realm. Then they started to look around the room it had purple wallpaper with some type of print on half of it, with the bottom half made of wood, a desk in the room, Plasma 90' inch T.V. with Wi-Fi mounted to the wall, a pullout couch which Joey put clam to, a bathroom which Sue had walked into. The bathroom had a mirror, same wallpaper as in the main room, a bathtub made of purple marble with a huge shower head that can massage you when you take a shower, some white and purple towels for both body and hands, a toilet made of purple marble as well with covers of plum purple, and a rug on the floor the same color as the cover on the toilet sit. Her month had dropped because she has never seen anything like this before. The Purple Plums Hotel was big on the color purple, but she was thinking it was more to do with the realm then the name of the hotel. Joey got comfortable on the couch and started to watch T.V. and was looking for a game of some kind and found a baseball game that was on with two teams he has never heard of. Sue got in the tub to relax, and they would then talk about how this was going to work and make plans to find the guardian of this realm. As the game was going on rooms service had called up to their room and asked what they would like to eat for dinner. Joey told them to bring up some crab, salad, soda, and desert to go with the dinner. After he got off the phone with room service Sue walked out of the bathroom in a purple night short outfit. He looked at her and smiled, he could see why Leroy fell for her when he met her at school. But thinking about his friends Lola, Rich, Alena, and Leroy just made him sad because he could not see them or spend time with them right now with their mission to find the other guardians'. Sue looked at him all funny and started to laugh because reminded her of when they were younger and how they stayed the night with each other, but then and now was way different because she was no longer a little girl, but a young lady and a powerful guardian.

"So, who was that on the phone?" Sue asked.

"Room service, wanted to know what we wanted for dinner, so I order for us if you don't mind." Joey said.

"No, I don't mind, thanks. Do you want to take a shower before we eat and start to make plans on how to find this guardian?" Sue asked.

"Yeah, here you can watch T.V. if you want to and use the card to pay for dinner okay. Just remember to sign MRS. RYAN, oaky." Joey said.

"Okay, I will remember." Sue said while laughing.

Joey went and got in the shower and Sue sat on the couch while finishing drying off from her long bath. Then there was a knock on the door, she got up and answered it. It was room service with dinner, and she took it in when she turned around, she realized that it had started to get dark and that the sky was turning a dark purple color with rain clouds coming in again.

"Oh, don't worry we have lightning rods on the top of the hotel so that the lightning doesn't strike and break everything." Room Service Guy said.

"Oh, okay. Thanks. How much do we own you?" Sue asked.

"It was charged to the room, so you don't have to pay anything." Room Service Guy said.

"Okay, thank you then. Bye." Sue said.

"Good night mam." Room Service Guy said.

As he walked out of the room, Joey had come out of the bathroom with a towel wrapped around his neck with purple night pants on. Sue looked at him and started to smile because she knew that she was not alone in this anymore.

"So ready to eat?" Sue asked.

"Yeah, I'm starved." Joey said laughing.

"Thanks for being here with me. Also don't you think it odd that we are no were near looking like we are 17 years old or adults; and that we are pretending to be married?" Sue asked.

"I think that teenagers can get married at very young age in this realm. All the people that we see come into this hotel that was couples looked no older than 16 years old, and that they are married." Joey said.

"Oh, well let us eat before our food gets cold because I'm hungry and I know that you are because we have not eaten since we left the Wind Realm." Sue said.

"Yeah, let's dig in." Joey said laughing.

As they ate their dinner of crab, salad, purple soda, and ice cream that was in the color of purple but tasted good. They started to talk about how they can look for the guardian of this realm and get access to the castle without being targeted for enemies. As they were finishing their dinner, they got this sense that something was about to happen or is going to happen. When they heard this loud bang, they turned around and looked out their windows and saw this huge ram like monster attacking the town they were in. As the monster ram got closer to the hotel, they notice that he was very big and was just as tall a skyscraper. It was time for them to act and they needed to because they could see people getting hurt in the street down below them.

"Let's go Sue." Joe said.

"Right behind you." Sue said.

As they ran for the elevator to get to the ground floor, they filet a trimmer which was not good, because the hotel started to shake. So, they ran back to their room and the monster ram was at their window breaking it and everything else that was in its path.

Chapter 12

As they reached their window it had be broken out and they needed to find a way to stop this monster from destroying everything. As it approached, they got ready to fight when someone had sent lightning at the ram, but they could not see who it was. As they looked on, they were not going to stand around and do nothing they wanted to help, so they called further their powers of Summoning and Light to help the person defending the people with their power.

"Light rings come to me." Sue called.

"I summon the Fire Dragon." Joey called

Joey and sue flew out of the window on the Fire Dragon to defeat the monster ram that was attacking the town. As they got near the monster ram, they started releasing their power on it, with the help from the lightning user they were able to bet the monster ram. As the fight ended it was already starting to get dawn outside with a million shades of purple in the sky. When they turned to say thank you to the lightning user the person was gone as if they were never there.

"Do you think that was the guardian of the Lightning Realm?" Sue asked.

"I'm not sure but got the feeling we will meet them again." Joey said.

Both had returned to the service desk and informed the sectary that the window in their room needed to be fixed due to the wired storm last night. So, the security offered them another room which was ten times bigger than their first one and at the same rate as the first room. This time the windows would be harder to break because they are bullet proof because it is the president or king suite which has the highest quaintly of security. This room had a living room, a bathroom with his and her towels, and sink for both, also a Jacuzzi tub for better relaxing time. The plasma T.V. was even bigger than the last one, it looks like a small theater screen in a movie theater. There were also movies and dvds that can be watched with a surround sound. The wallpaper was the same as their first room which was pretty much standard compared to this room. The bed even seemed to be a lot bigger than the last one. As Sue was walking around the room to see all the things that might be difference, she also notices things that were the same which made it odder than a cat being able to talk. Joey was looking out the window to see and wonder how they could look for the next guardian so it came to him he chooses to rent a car, but first he would have to run it by Sue first. If she goes for it, they can pretend to be going on a drive through the country and start their search for the next guardian of the Lightning Realm.

"Sue, would you like to go on a drive through the country tomorrow?" Joey asked.

"Yeah, that sounds like fun, and we can start looking for the Lightning Guardian." Sue said.

"Good, then let's get some sleep for a few hours and then go on the trip, okay." Joey said.

"Okay wills I'm going to sleep for a few hours then maybe we can head out." Sue said.

As the two dozed off for a few hours because they asked the front desk for a wakeup call and then Joey also requested a car with a drop top, he also had clothes brought up to them that he found on the computer and order. He orders Sue a Summer Dress which is the color of light purple with white flower print on it, he got himself a pair of cotton pants that were the same color as Sue's dress with a short sleeve button up white shirt. As she came out of the bathroom Joey pointed to a wrapped gift that was sitting on the table. Sue walked over to it and started to open; when she finally got the box opened, she pulled out the summer dress and her face lighted up. Then she took in Joey and notice that he was changed in clothes she has never seen on him before.

"Don't you look hot?" Sue said laughing.

"Thanks, and you are gonna look stunning in that summer dress. I was thinking we take a ride into the country and start our search for the guardian." Joey said with a smile.

"Okay let me get changed, and then we will go. But how will get there?" Sue asked.

"I order a car for us to take into the country for a little country ride as a couple even though it is a cover, I don't want anyone to discover we are guardians before we find the 7th guardian. Most of all it might just through off the Dark Kingdom Zodiac off our trail for a while." Joey said.

"Got ya. I understand it would be nice to be able to just look for the n0065t guardian and not have to keep looking over our shoulders every time we turn around." Sue said.

"Sue we still need to keep our guard up." Joey said.

"Okay." Sue said.

As she walked into the bathroom to change into her new summer dress which it seemed so long ago that she was at the dance with her friends and buying a new dress for their dance. It had been months since they left the Crystal Star of Water and Ice. Also, it only has been a few days now since she had sent Rich and Lola to the Crystal Realm of Water and Ice. She so much wanted to show Alena and Lola her new dress, only wish they could enjoy it with her. It is fun being with Joey after all these years, but sometimes it is good just to have a girl talk, hang out with friends and talk about boys, clothes, what they are going to do over the summer, but most of all she missed her best friends. She knew it was the good of having peace again when all the guardians are found and then the Star Princess will be found. So, she walked out of the bathroom she looked stunning in her new dress. Joey looked away from the window and looked at Sue and he smiled. His cousin had grown into a very young woman.

"You look good." Joey said.

"Thanks, you good too." Sue said.

"Are you ready to go the car is waiting?" Joey said.

"Yeah, lets' get this show on the road." Sue said.

The two went to the elevator and headed down to the 1st floor and out the front doors of the hotel. As they stepped out the car was waiting for them it was a hot rod with a drop top in the color of pink and purple. Sue's mouth dropped as she seen the car. She knew that Joey had money but didn't think he had this much money. She knew that Joey's dad had money and plus what they got from the car accident that cost him his mother and brother when he was younger. As they got into the car, they took off to the country to look for the guardian of this realm.

As they are driving, they stop to eat at this park type that was made of nothing but flowers. These flowers were the same color as the ones they had seen in town, but there was more of them than in the town. There were purple roses, violet tulips, dark purple irises, plum daisies, and light purple lilies. Sue was walking through the field of all kinds of purple flowers as she stopped, she picked a dark purple iris which then started to shimmer and as she was holding the dark purple iris it shocked her like static electricity from another person or clothes. Sue had dropped the iris and as she did it started to get bigger as if someone gave it miracle grow. It had teeth the size of trash cans. As she is moving back the iris starts to advance on her she called for her power, but it did not work. It was like the iris sucked her power from her and it made the flower grow. Joey came running and as he approached the iris started to advance on him Joey was able to summon the Fire Dragon and the iris burned up to a crisp. Sue had fallen to her knees and just started to cry. Joey held her for a good hour while she just let it out. She was missing home, her friends, her family, even her annoying little brother. Joey knew how she felt because he felt the same way she does now when his father took him away from her when they were younger. He also missed his friends now.

"Come on, get up and wrap your face." Joey said.

Sue did as he asked and she did feel better after just being able to let go and not have to worry about being made fun of, by people walking by. They got back into the car and were driving again through the country, and then they notice a person walking on the side of the road by them self. Joey was coming near the person when a guest of wind just hit them, and the car went out of control. Joey was able to steady the car before it could get out of control. He looked at Sue and saw the worry on her face. She was thinking the same thing he was.

"That guest of wind didn't come from just anywhere." Sue said.

"Yeah, you are right. We need to get off the road before something worse happens." Joey said.

"Agreed." Sue said.

As they start to pull off the road another guest of wind came at them, and it was stronger than the last guest of wind. As this wind hit them, they went sliding on the ground, but beforehand they notice there was a cliff nearby and that was where the car was heading. As it reached the edge of the cliff they jumped from the car and landed on the ground only for Sue to slip and go over the cliff. Joey grabbed her and was holding onto her when she went swinging over the edge.

"Please don't drop me." Sue screamed.

"I'm not going to let go. So don't give up. I'm going to pull you up so hold on." Joey screamed back.

As Joey was holding onto Sue he started to cry because he didn't want to lose her gain after finding his cousin again. It had been years since he seen her, and he was not about to let her go now. They were in this together, so he held on, and she started to slip from his grip. So, he used both hands to hold on to her while lying on the ground among the purple flowers. Then another gust of wind came at them, and Joey was barely holding on to Sue. As the wind had passed over them Joey felt an evil that was in the wind. He knew the Dark Kingdom Zodiac was going to make the guardians pay for everything they had lost in the last few months because of the will of fire to protect their friends and family.

"Sue please; hold on." Joey yelled.

"I'm trying but my hands are started to slip out of yours." Sue yelled back.

"I'm not letting go so you don't either." Joey screamed over the howl of the wind.

As the wind died down again, but it seemed that the winds keep getting stronger that the last one. They were trying to kill them, and Joey knew this. Sue felt it to. As the next wind hit them this time Sue lost her grip and she started to fall, and Joey couldn't grab her. Then someone was next to him with violet hair, amber eyes, and her face was different. It was the person from the lightning field, from the other day. She had grabbed Sue by the hand and was pulling her up only to slip again.

"Thank you so much." Joey said.

"Quit the small talk and help me pull her up before that evil guest of wind hits us again." Female girl said.

"Okay." Joey said.

He reached down and grabbed Sue's hand and between him the girl they were able to get Sue over the edge next to them. As she got back over the edge she rolled onto her back and breathing hard. Joey was wiping the tears from his eyes because he came close to losing someone very close to his heart. He was glad that they sent Rich and Lola back because he could not bear to lose either of them. He looked over at Sue and the girl and she was sitting up only to be staring at something that was looking at them. As Joey had looked up, he notices that there was someone coming near them, and the person didn't seem friendly at all.

"Well done guardians and princess." The Joker said.

"YOU!!" Princess Faizah Carter said.

"Don't look so upset princess. We only wanted your loyalty and your realm." The Joker said.

"Guardians welcome to the Crystal Star of the Lightning Realm. Meet the Princess of this realm Princess Faizah Carter." The Joker said.

"How dare you show your wicked face hear. This is the field of my ancestors." Princess Faizah said.

"You, we saw you on the road into town." Sue said.

"Tell me where you the one that sent that monster size ram into the town hurting all those people." Joey said.

"All don't be upset with my welcome present for you two guardians. Princess met the guardian and Prince of the Crystal Star of Summoning Joseph Ryan, and his partner the guardian and Princess of the Crystal Star of Light and Travel Sue Stang. Where are the other two guardians?" The Joker asked.

"That is none of your business." Sue said.

"Ah, don't be like that we can all be friends here." The Joker said.

"Not on your life pal." Sue said.

"Come on Princess Sue, it would give me great pleasure to see you all suffer, but if and when you do make it to the castle of this realm, I have some gifts for all of you, but don't think that it is going to be a walk through the park to get there either." The Joker said.

"Get lost creep." Princess Faizah said.

As she said this the Joker had disappeared into the mist rising from the flowers. She didn't seem like a bad person; but she needed to get back to the castle to help her parents, but she knew she also had a spiritual journey to do to earn her powers, but something seems to keep getting in the way.

Chapter 13

"I'm sorry, but I can't help you two out. I was just walking by when I saw that the car went over the cliff. My name is Faizah Carter, I'm 18 years old, I'm the princess of the Lightning and its' next guardian in line for the throne. I don't have my powers yet because in my family we must prove we are brave, caring, strong, and loving. "Faizah said.

"It is nice to meet you, my name is Sue Stang. I'm 15, getting ready to turn 16 years old on June 15. Please just call me Sue." Sue said.

"We understand, but if there is chance can we go a little was with you or at least until we can get to the town or city. My name is Joseph Ryan, 16 years old, I just turned 16 in March. Please call me Joey. We are the guardians of the Majestic Star Kingdom." Joey said.

"I know about the Majestic Star Kingdom, my family has been protecting that kingdom for centuries, we have heard rumors that there is a chance that the Star Princess is still alive." Faizah said.

"Oh, please don't get it wrong we just learned that we are guardians of our own realms and that the Star Princess is alive we just must find her, and the only way to do that is to gather all the guardians' again to release her powers. We have found the Prince of the Elemental Realm." Sue said.

"WHAT!! You have found the Prince of the Crystal Star of the Elemental Realm." Faizah said.

"Yeah, his name is Leroy Addams. He is right now on the Crystal Star of Water and Ice with three other guardians." Joey said.

"Then we will have to work together. If you can help me, I can help you." Faizah said.

"You got it." Sue said.

Faizah could not believe what she was hearing. The prince has already been found. Which means that the Dark Kingdom Zodiac must know as well, she was thinking. How can the Price be protected only by three guardians? But what Faizah didn't know was that the prince is a guardian himself. His job was to protect his true love from all harm, and he had failed because they were attacked without warning. From what Faizah had learned from her family is that the Star Princess and Prince would bring peace, love, and prosperity to all the realms, and they would be better rulers than the ones before. She was always told that she had to find the Star Princess on her own. She has learned not trust anyone because they would turn on you if the price is right. She learned this lesson the hard way because her best friend had turned on her because she was promised that she could become Queen and found out she was tricked in turning her best friend over to the Dark Kingdom Zodiac.

"Faizah, can you tell us more about the Majestic Star Kingdom?" Sue asked.

"What do you want to know?" Faizah said.

"Well, Joey and I are on this mission to find all the guardians', so we can find the Star Princess. From what we have learned from the other guardians' that we have met and made friends with, also from the two protectors?" Sue said.

"Two protectors? You mean they have finally showed themselves." Faizah said.

"What do you mean about showing themselves?" Sue asked.

"The protectors had gone into hiding until they could find the first and maybe the most powerful guardian that ever was born." Faizah said.

"Well Jennifer and Glen found Alena before me, and Joey had already known he was a guardian because Jennifer had found him when he was 12 years old." Sue said.

"They have found her. Which means the prince is in good hands of being protected from the Dark Kingdom." Faizah.

"It isn't Leroy who needed to be protected from the dark kingdom it was Alena because the Dark Prince Jordan wants to marry her and try and take her from us." Sue said.

138

"If her loyalties can be swayed then she needs to go and can't be trusted." Faizah said.

"Let me tell you something, first Alena would not betray her friends, she fought by herself for weeks, and she is the most loyal person you could ever met. Not only that what made you so cold hearted and not trust anybody." Sue said with angry.

"You don't even know me, so how can you judge me?" Faizah said.

"By your attitude that is how. You have been hurt I understand that, but sometimes we must trust those we don't want to. If we can't trust, then we all might as well go over to the Dark Kingdom Zodiac because they would have already won." Sue said.

Sue went a head of Faizah steaming over there conversation about this and about that. She could not see what her problem was, but she just doesn't have a clue on how we can bet the Dark Kingdom Zodiac if a guardian doesn't have trust, love, or even friendship. All she wanted to do was become friends with her, but it doesn't look like they would be able to. So, Sue just walked a head of her and Joey. Joey had walked up next to Faizah and started to talk to her.

"Please forgive Sue, Alena and she have been best friends since childhood and when you bad mouth talk one her friends, she gets very upset. See, Sue don't have many friends in her life because of growing up with powers, people made fun of her all the time, until one day Alena Patches came to school.

Alena and her mother had just moved to Sunny Ville, Ohio after her father had died in an accident at work. Well Sue was being picked on and Alena stood up for her. So, they have been best friends since." Joey said.

"I'm sorry, I don't mean to be rude or mean to her. It must be nice to have a loyal friend like that." Faizah said.

"Yeah, Alena would give her life for Sue and all her friends because she has already done that by protecting her from many attacks that has happened since she found out she was a guardian." Joey said.

"They never knew they were guardians' destined to protect the Star Princess and Prince." Faizah said.

"No, they just found out. Alena took it well, but Sue didn't until she learned that Alena was in trouble." Joey said.

"What kind of trouble did Alena get into?" Faizah asked

"She was kidnapped by the Dark Kingdom, and they were trying to force her to marry the Dark Prince, but she would not give in. Alena is very strong and pure hearted." Joey said.

"Why would the Dark Kingdom take her? The Dark Prince was supposed to marry the Star Princess by force if they needed to, but her heart was with someone else." Faizah said.

"Well, the Dark Prince said since the Star Princess was lost in the battle for the Majestic Star Kingdom, the next in line would be the most powerful guardian and that was the guardian of the

Crystal Star Realm of Water and Ice. That guardian is Alena." Joey said.

"You sound like you know her? Like you have known her your whole life." Faizah said.

"I dated that guardian. I do know her; her heart is as pure as snow. She is very beautiful and loving." Joey said.

"What does she look like?" Faizah said.

"Hair as dark as a raven's feather, skin color of a light tan, her eyes are light brown to honey color, with a little hint of green, and she stands 5'2". She is 15 years old, she is in high school, and she will be 16-year-old on October 20th." Joey said.

"It sounds like she is very pretty." Faizah said.

As they are walking in silence, with Sue a head of them. Joey was wondering why Faizah seemed to be holding back and keeping people at bay. It is as she has been very hurt in the past. This would make since with her remarks to Sue about Alena. Joey wasn't sure if this was a good thing for the guardians or even for Faizah if she wanted to be the next guardian of this realm because she must be able to get past the hurt in her heart for her to even gain her powers from her family. As they kept walking down the road, they were coming upon a town which seemed to be a good thing because they were all feeling tired and hungry.

"Here is the town you asked me to take you two too." Faizah said.

"Thanks for the help. Do you think we can keep traveling together for a little bit longer, because we need to find out information about the next realm we need to find. Also, we need to find a way that realm as well. Sue can open a portal into that realm if there is something connecting us to it." Joey asked.

"Well, let me think about it? I do think I could use some sleep after the day we have had." Faizah said.

"That will be fine. Do you have any idea if there is a place to rest at in the town?" Joey asked.

"Yeah, I think that we can stay at my family's estate for the night." Faizah said.

"That would be great. Thank you so much." Joey said.

"You're welcome." Faizah said.

"SUE!!!" Joey yelled at her.

Sue turned around and then before she could sense it something hit her in the back, when she was about to yell back at Joey. Joey and Faizah ran over to her, she was out cold. As they had reached her something came flying past their heads. Joey rolled to his left as Faizah had rolled to her right out of the path of another attack. Joey was holding onto Sue and when he turned around something was coming at them fast. Faizah was stunned to see it was her best friend now a general in the Dark Kingdom Zodiac.

"Lynn what are you doing?" Faizah said.

"Well Princess, I have gain powers that would make you look like nothing. I also have been promised to become the Queen of this realm and your family is finished." Lynn said.

"How could you do this? Are you that jealous of my family and me for you to do to this?" Faizah asked.

"Well, you did always act like you were better than me." Lynn said.

"I have never acted like that. You know I hated the fact that was of royal blood." Faizah said.

"Yeah right, it doesn't matter now because you will kneel to me now and forever." Lynn said laughing.

"Please don't do this? I beg of you. Lynn you can still be saved just let go of your hatred for the royal family please." Faizah begged.

"Why would I do that? I'm loving this; it is like nothing I have ever felt before. I am quite enjoying it." Lynn said.

"Why, we were best friends." Faizah started to cry.

As Joey was starting to get on his feet, he saw that Faizah and the general was in a heavy conversation and it seemed they know each other very well. As Joey was looking onto the scene, he notices that Faizah was crying, but most of all her shoulder was bleeding. He looked at Sue and she seemed to be okay, no damage done was just knocked out. So, Joey laid Sue down, and ran to help Faizah.

"Faizah what is going on?" Joey yelled while running to her.

She looked in his direction and she yelled back.

"Joey stay away, don't come any closer." Faizah yelled at him.

"NO!! I am coming." Joey said.

"Who is this Faizah a new boyfriend? He is quite good looking." Lynn said.

"No, he is not my boyfriend. I just met him." Faizah said.

"Too bad because you never know when something that good comes around. I might have to make him my play toy." Lynn said laughing.

"You are sick. What have you done to yourself?" Faizah asked.

"I have done nothing, but it was good when I got the chance to be with Dark Prince in his bed. It was different, but good." Lynn said.

"You are sick. How could you do that? What were you thinking?" Faizah asked.

"I had to give up my purity to gain this power and it was by far the best choice ever. Now I'm going to kill the last blood line of the royal family of the Crystal Star of Lightning Realm." Lynn said.

"What does that have to do with me?" Faizah said.

"You are dense. You were not told anything of your birth were you." Lynn said.

"What does my birth have anything to do with the royal family or you for that matter?" Faizah asked.

"You are the last blood of the royal family. With your blood running out then there wouldn't be anyone from the Lightning Realm to help the guardians out or have anyone left from the royal family to rule this realm so the Dark Kingdom Zodiac to take over and rule." Lynn said.

"I won't let that happen. You will have to kill me first." Faizah said.

"It can be arranged." Lynn said with an evil grain.

Chapter 14

"Lynn how could you do that? I loved you from the first day I met you. We became really good friends." Faizah said.

"You loved me. Please, I saw how you would look at every guy that came into the room. Also, when I asked Jim Conner, he told me no because he wanted you. He wanted all of you. So why should I be second to you, because you are of royal blood, beautiful, tall, and dark skin." Lynn said with angry.

"I was never interested in him. I turned him down because I know you really liked him." Faizah said.

"Really, then why did he sleep with me and turn around and ask you out. He told me that you asked him out, and that you wanted to get together." Lynn said.

"He lied to you, I never did anything with him, and he was not my type." Faizah said.

"So now he isn't good enough for you?" Lynn asked.

"It is not like that I don't date guys." Faizah said.

"I'm broad with this conversation let get this over with." Lynn said.

"Fine then let us get this over with." Faizah said.

"What can you do? You don't even have your powers yet, because you have not finished your spiritual journey." Lynn said laughing.

Joey had reached Faizah and looked between her and this person. What was going on Faizah was crying, holding her shoulder and looked as if she had been slapped in the face. She looked pale and her eyes seemed to change color from violet to a dark purple.

"Faizah who is this? What does she want with you?" Joey asked.

"You ask who I am. Then let me tell you handsome. I'm General Lynn Davies of the Dark Kingdom Zodiac and going to be the Queen of this realm once she is gone." Lynn said.

"Well first my name is Joseph Ryan; I am the guardian of summons to the Crystal Star of Summons. What do you want with Faizah?" Joey said.

"Oh, I have been told about you. I am guessing that the girl I hit early with my spike she is a guardian too. She isn't much of a guardian if I can take her down like that." Lynn said.

Sue was starting to come to when she heard Joey talking to someone. Her head hurt bad, but she did not seem to be bleeding at all. As she sat up, she looked over at Joey and Faizah. Someone was there with them, who was it? Then she saw the general attack them. With looked like a spike the size of a tree branch.

"I call my powers to me." Lynn called.

"I summon the Dragon of lightning." Joey called.

As General Lynn attacked Faizah, Joey had scooped her up on the dragon and Lynn had missed. She throws another spike at them this time it hit Joey in the left shoulder. Sue was watching in the background feeling dazed from being hit with one of those spikes. She knew she needed to help her cousin and Faizah.

"Light Rings come to me. Wrap her up." Sue called.

Before Lynn could see the attacked, she was wrapped in a rope of light holding her in place. She could not move and when she looked up, she saw Sue in the background using her powers. Joey had looked where Lynn was looking at and saw that Sue was awake. He also took the chance to attack Lynn while Sue was holding, and not being sure how long she can hold her, he let Lynn have it.

"Lightning Dragon let her have it." Joey said.

A lightning bolt hit Lynn. As it hit her, she screams with pain, and feel to her knees. As she did this Sue let the Light Rings go and clasped again from using her powers in her condition. Joey had the Lightning Dragon land and Faizah ran to Lynn as she hit the ground. As she was holding her Faizah starting to cry, Lynn looked up at her.

"Why are you crying? I deserve this; I don't deserve your pity. You where my best friend and I am sorry. As Lynn had dropped her head, her eyes closed, and she started to disappear into dust. As she turned to dust Faizah just closed her hands around herself and really started to cry. Joey walked over to her, he felt bad for what happened, and he knew the sadness very well. He put his hands around Faizah and just held her and she cried and cried for what seemed forever. When she finally stopped, she looked at him and she realized that there are people worth fighting for, most of all for her friends. She owned Sue an apology for her actions. As she was pulling herself together, she looked at Joey. She smiled at him and knew that she found some good friends in both him and Sue.

"Thank you for letting me is myself." Faizah said.

"It is not a problem. That is what friends are for. We need to have each other's back no matter what." Joey said.

"I do own Sue an apology. All she was trying to do was get to know me and wanted to be friends. I think that everyone has problems that have to be dealt with before they can move on." Faizah said.

"Yeah, we do. She will get over being mad. She wasn't going to let anything happen to us if she could help it. So how about we get a move on to your family's estate and get off this road. I do think that Sue is going to need some time to recover from her injuries." Joey said.

"Yeah, I think so to. We can stay at my family's estate for a couple of days. I would also like to talk to you both about this spiritual journey I'm on to gain my powers." Faizah said.

"Sounds good, we can talk at the estate, and make plans from there. You can also explain what all you have to do for this spiritual journey you are on." Joey said.

"Okay, the estate is at the other side of the town up ahead." Faizah said.

"What is the name of the town?" Joey asked.

"It is called Cherry Blossom Village." Faizah said.

"Is there a reason it is called that? Does it have purple flowers as well?" Joey asked.

"It is called Cherry Blossom Village because the most cherry trees grow in this town all year around. No, they are not purple even though that is the natural color of this realm, they happen to be pale pink." Faizah said while laughing.

"Oh, sorry I just assumed that every flower is purple because that is all that we have seen since we got here." Joey said.

"It is okay, it is the natural color of most flowers, but there are a few that are different. Well should we get Sue and be on our way." Faizah said.

"Yeah." Joey said.

As the two walked over to Sue who had passed out from pain and using her powers. Joey picked Sue up and carried her, the rest of the way to village. As they entered the town everyone was walking by and stopped and bowed to Faizah. Joey looked around and he seen Cherry Blossoms blowing in the nice summer breeze. Joey also had notice that it seemed warmer in the village than outside it.

"Don't be shocked, every time a person walks into the village, they notice the temperature change between the bolder of the village and outside the village. My estate is on the other side of the village; all we must do is take the main road to my family home. It is maybe about a 10-minute walk from the entrance of the village." Faizah said.

"It must show on my face, the shock. Okay please lead the way." Joey said.

As the three went through the village to Faizah's family estate Joey had notice that the village was way different than the ones he has been in since they left the Crystal Star of the Water and Ice Realm. He was taking everything in as they walked, he notices that there was a mixture of different color flowers as they walked through town. Some of the shops seemed to sell the widest things. From chicken feet to bat wings to flowers they have never seen before.

"What kind of village is this?" Joey asked.

"The village is made up of those people who can tap into the powers of this realm, or some cases it is called "magic" which are most likely the word you would use. These people use this stuff for many things, they can case spells that can heal, or cause death to a person who has done wrong. My family built this village for those people who showed a chance of being able to use magic or even use the Lightning powers of this realm, which in most people is very hard unless they have the royal blood line in them somewhere down the line. I do have cousins here that can only use part of the royal bloodline powers. But still we ran here when the Dark Kingdom attacked our realm and my home. So be careful not to say the name of the Dark Kingdom's name because these people would most likely become hostile to you. They can see that you have powers too, but not of this realm. They also can see that both Sue and you have pure hearts." Faizah said.

"Thanks for the warning, we will be careful. So, each person hear can use power from healing to lightning." Joey said.

"Yeah. It is hard to become a magic user, most people try all there life to be accepted into the Academy of Magic. That is our school in this realm. It goes from pre-school to college if we want to continue our training in the magic arts, or when it is time for our spiritual journey. Which is what I am on, I had been attending the Academy of Magic up until my 18th birthday which I just had. In the royal family when we hit a certain age, we must undergo a spiritual journey that is more difficult than the normal spiritual journey kids that are not part of the royal family takes. Using the magic calls to you, for me it had been calling to me for years, but it was not time to take that journey yet. Most kids go to the

Academy of Magic until the start of their third or fourth year in the college part. Do you have a school you attend?" Faizah asked.

"It sounds like each realm is different in many things. Yes, we do but our schools are spilt up into four types: there is grade school which holds our pre-school – fourth grade, middle school which holds our 5-8th grades, high school which holds our 9-12th grades, and then if you choose to you can go to college which has many ranges. The name of the high school Sue, Leroy, Alena, and I go too is called Sunny Ville High School." Joey said.

"It sounds like you have many choices to choose from. Sometimes I wish that was here. You are right; each realm is different when it comes to education. Well, here we are." Faizah said.

Joey looked up and realized that they had reached the estate. He must of not notice because of them talking about school. Joey seemed to miss school as well, because he got to see his friends all the time.

The estate had many flowers mostly purple; he assumed that is because they are the royal family. There were other flowers of different colors, different sizes, and different shapes. Here carried Sue through the gate to the estate and into the front door. As he enters the house, he stopped in the doorway and his month dropped because the house was bigger than his. Then they are the royal family of this realm so appearance must be a big thing for them. He walked the rest of the way into the house and laid Sue on the couch. Faizah went and found some glazes for Sue's head, and clean wash clothes to put a cool rag on her forehead to see if that will help.

"You have a nice house; if you can call it a house it is bigger than my high school." Joey said.

"Thanks, it is for show, and my parents wanted to make sure we had enough room for people when they visited, for parties, and just in case there was an emergency we can help the people out with a place to lay their head if they lose their homes for one reason or another." Faizah said.

"At least your parents were thinking of the people in those cases." Joey said.

"Yeah, the people say they are the best rulers they have ever seen in this realm for many years." Faizah said.

As they were talking Sue started to wake up with a splitting headache. With Joey and Faizah standing over her. She looked around and she realized that they were no longer on the road.

"Where are we?" Sue asked.

"You are at my house." Faizah said.

"Oh, okay. Do you have any headache pills, my head hurts really bad?" Sue asked.

"Yeah, let me get you some." Faizah said.

"Thanks." Sue said.

"Welcome. Sue I'm sorry for the way I acted on the way here." Faizah said.

"I understand how you might be feeling when someone that you are close to, and they hurt you very badly." Sue said.

"Yeah, well that does not make excuse for my action and how I treated you. Right now, it will be hard to trust about anybody. So, if you don't mind, I would like to become friends, just don't ask me to trust you right now." Faizah said.

"That is okay with me. We can work on the trust thing as time goes on. I would like to become really good friends." Sue said.

"Me, too." Faizah said with a smile.

"Aww, don't you two sound sweet." Joey said laughing.

The girls joined in with the laughing and it looked like they could become good friends in the end. After joking around with each other and laughing until they had tears in their eyes. They sat down and ate some food and went off to bed to get some well-earned sleep. They had plan on heading out after breakfast the next morning if Sue was feeling a lot better. Faizah had called in a healer to heal Sue from one of the healers that have served the royal family for many years. As the healer came, he looked at Sue and smiled. He had healed her and told both Faizah and Joey to let Sue sleep for a while and he would be back in the morning to check on her before breakfast. They agreed to that and giving her some food and time to rest would be good for her.

Chapter 15

⋇⋇⋇⋇⋇◦⋇⋇⋇⋇⋇

The healer returned that following morning to check on Sue as he looks her over, he had given her a clear clean release of health. He walked over to Faizah and told her that Sue was going to be okay that she only had a big knot on her head from falling early that day. That was the excuse they gave the healer when he looked at Sue and asked her what had hurt. They didn't want to tell the healer the truth, so they could just avoid answering a lot of questions about his and about that, what is a guardian, and many other questions that had popped into their heads when telling the healer what had happened. As they ate breakfast on the patio, they had eggs of all kinds, orange juice, milk, coffee, muffins of all kinds as well, and all kinds of fruit that was in season. As they ate Sue was looking around and she saw roses, tulips, lilies, irises, daisies, and other flowers she could not name off the top of her head. The patio was nice with a patio table set, wood burner, fire ring to roast hot dogs, marshmallows, and so on. The table was Purple/White, comfortable sits, and a glass table. There was also a set of chairs with comfortable sits, and a love sit that was the same color as the main table set. The was so big that it had at least 12 bathrooms, 20 guest rooms, and a huge dining room with a table the length of the room that was made up of solid wood. So, they sat and ate and were enjoying the view they had. Faizah gave Sue some nice traveling clothes and gave Joey a nice pair of jeans and nice shirt to ware. As they are getting ready to head out Faizah stopped in the doorway and looked at the two and started to smile.

"Before we head out, I need to let you know that when we leave town, we are going to have to ride horseback though the rest of the country because there are no roads from here out until you reach the capital where the royal family lives and the castle is located." Faizah said.

"Okay, I have no problem riding horseback because my family would take trips to go riding." Sue said.

"Well, my dearest cousin may have ridden a horse before and many times too, but I have never ridden a horse in my whole entire life." Joey said.

"It isn't that hard; just make sure you keep your legs close to the horse's body and hold on to the rains really tit because you don't want to fall off. That would hurt a lot and it could make you lose your memory for a little bit." Faizah said.

"Yeah, it isn't hard to learn to ride or fall off." Sue said laughing.

"You are not very funny." Joey said.

"So now that you know that, let us be on our way. As we reach the end of town that is where we will get the horses for our trip into the capital." Faizah said.

"Okay." Joey and Sue said.

As they left the estate and headed for the end of town, they seen many places that good animals, but no horses. Joey and Sue where started to wonder if they were ever getting a horse before they left town. As they had reached the end of town, someone was waiting for them with three horses. As Faizah walked up to the man and took the horses from him and handed one to Sue and one to Joey she looked back at the man.

"Thank you for the help." Faizah said.

"You are much welcome princess. I own a lot to your father for helping me when I needed it most." Guy said.

"Well take care and I hope we can see each other again soon." Faizah said.

"Me as well." Guy said.

As they were leaving the town Faizah turned around and was waving bye to the guy that was standing at the edge of town. He had waved back praying she and her new friends have a safe trip into the capital. As they were out of sight of the town, they turned down one dirt side road to get supplies they would need. It was a whole day's ride to the capital with the short cuts that Faizah knows. This would make it a lot easier for them to keep out sight from the Dark Kingdom Zodiac.

As they have neared the capital it was almost dusk now and the gates would be coming down soon if they did not make it there soon. As they approached the capital a guard stopped them from entering the capital.

"State your business." Guard said.

"It is I Princess Faizah. I have returned from my spiritual journey. Please let my friends and me pass into the capital we have business with the Queen and King." Faizah said.

"Your highness we heard that you were dead." Guard said.

"Who told you I was dead?" Faizah said with anger

"It was the persist from the Pillar Town, right off the road from the lightning field." Guard said.

"Then he has lied to you and the people of the capital. How are my parents doing?" Faizah said.

"Your mother has been bed ridding due to the news she heard, and the baby is not doing so well either. Your father has not left the capital for days because of losing you." Guard said.

"Then I think we need to make a visit to the castle to clear up this little miss understanding." Faizah said.

"But my lady, your parents put the persist in charge of everything that has to do with the welfare of the people including security. He gave order not let anyone in who looked like you because he said it was an imposter." Guard said.

"Then tell me do you think I'm an imposter?" Faizah asked.

"No, my lady because only the royal family can ride those horses and obeys their command. If anyone that was not of royal blood can't ride that horse like you do. I'm guessing the two that are with you are not from this realm but have royal blood that served the Majestic Star Kingdom, because only those who have served the great kingdom can ride those horses as well." Guard said.

"You are right, they are of royal blood line that served the great kingdom, but also has met the prince and is looking for the guardians that will serve them loyal, well, and true." Faizah said.

"Then my lady I will let you past but take the secret tunnel to your room. Then go to the throne to prove your worth to your parents." Guard said whiling bowing them into the capital.

"Thank you. I will prove myself to them all." Faizah said.

So, the two guardians and Faizah rode into the capital to an area that looked like it could be overlooked if you did not look close enough. As they approached the area Sue notice that there was an opening going underground to a tunnel. As they walked up to it; it started to shimmer with flowers of purple that looked like mist and created a light glow on the floor so they could see where they were walking. As the tunnel came to an end at another door with a combination lock on it, they notice that it took them an hour to get through the tunnel as Faizah put in the combination the door opened into a huge room that could fit at the less a hundred people.

"I'm sorry but we can't stay here we need to get to the throne room before my father gives up his hold on our kingdom over to the Dark Kingdom Zodiac." Faizah said.

"Not a problem. How far is the throne room from here?" Joey asked.

"It is only a few minutes from here. You don't have to go with me, this is my fight." Faizah said.

"You are wrong there. It is our fight, and we go together that is what friends do for each other. So, we are not letting you go by yourself. End of conversation." Sue said.

"Then thank you for your help. We can get there faster is we run." Faizah said.

"You got it." Joey said.

As the three ran down the hall and turned a corner to enter the throne room there was something in their way. It looked like guards, which made it hard for them to pass. They went over to the guards and Faizah demined them to move, but they refused to do as she said. They were in a dazed like someone had put a spell on them and not to obey orders. So, Joey and Sue knocked them out and they pulled the doors open to the throne room and ran in.

"Stop this as once!" Faizah said.

"On who's orders?" Persist asked.

"On mine the princess of this realm and this castle." Faizah said.

"Is that really you my dearest daughter and heir to the throne of our beloved kingdom?" King asked.

"Yes, father it really is me. This man has told you lies about me, and he is trying to take over our kingdom for the Dark Kingdom Zodiac." Faizah said.

"Thank the gods, you are safe." King said.

"It would seem that; that damned Lynn failed in her mission to kill you three." Persist said.

"It would seem that you are out of place here." Joey said stepping up next to Faizah with his spear in hand.

"So, tell us who you really then?" Sue said walking up next to Joey and Faizah with her twin swords in hand.

"Where did you guys get those weapons from?" Faizah asked.

"They were gifts from the guardian of the Crystal Star of Fire Realm. We have had them, but they have been in between space and time thanks to Joey's light dragon who has been carrying our stuff for us since we left the Crystal Star of Water and Ice." Sue said.

"It would have been nice to know this." Faizah said.

"Sorry, with everything that has happened we forgot to tell you." Joey said.

"That is fine for now; we need to deal with this creep here." Faizah said.

"So, tell me princess what do you intend to do?" Persist said.

"First you can drop the act I know you are no Persist, and second we are going to wipe the floor with you." Faizah said.

"Please don't be like this. You have no chance of betting me without your powers princess." Persist said.

"You are wrong there. Faizah looks deep inside the power has always been with you, but there are certain things that the royal family must go through before they can gain that power." King said.

"What would that be?" Faizah asked.

"You had to suffer hard ship, lost, love, and friendship to gain your powers." King said.

"But have I felt all those things." Faizah asked.

"Enough of this talking. Dark Lightning come to me." Persist said.

"You are not a persist, you are the Joker one of the generals of the Dark Kingdom Zodiac." Sue said.

"Way to go guardian of light and travel." Joker said.

"I call fourth the dragon of earth." Joey said.

"Light rings come to me." Sue said.

As the two guardians called fourth their powers the Joker hit them with such power that it sent them flying through the throne room. The king stood up and used his powers over the lightning and sent a lightning bolt at the general. As the bolt hit the Joker, he had fell to his knees just to send an even more powerful attack at the king. Faizah fell to her knees crying at her father's side holding him because she felt so useless, her friends where hurt because of her, and now her father is near death. What can she do to help? Was she always this week? These things ran though her head as the Joker sent another attack at her. All she could do was sit there and watch but something happened the attack did not hit her instead it hit Sue who though herself in front of Faizah to protect her with a light shield only to still be hit with the attack causing her to fall. Faizah caught her.

"Why, would protect me after what I have said to you?" Faizah asked.

"Because that is what friends do for each other. We protect those we love and care about." Sue said, and then she passed out in Faizah's arms.

"That is, it I have had with the likes of you and your kind, you hurt my friends, and put my father on his death bed, and now my kingdom and me might be facing slavery from you. I WON'T STAND FOR THIS ANYMORE!!!" Faizah said with anger.

Then something had happened she felt this warmth in her body and then she senses the lightning all over the realm bending to her will, her hatred, her pain, and the most of emotion the desire to save those she loves. She smiled at the Joker when we realized that he no longer had control over the realms power.

"Lightning Storm come to me. With all the lightning in this realm, get rid of the Joker who poses a threat to our beautiful realm, and the people living here." Faizah called.

The Joker had felt the power of the lightning come though his power and exploding him from the inside out, turning the Joker to dust. Faizah ran to her father and held him. Joey was getting up and walked over to Sue who start to wake from the attack which did not cause as much damage as thought and they both walked over to where Faizah was sitting holding her father.

"You did it my daughter. You found the power inside of you. My daughter with all my love you become the guardian of the Crystal Star of Lightning. Please find the other guardians', the prince, and the Star Princess to bring peace to all the realms. Guardian of Light and Travel, I knew your birth parents and they were very strong indeed, but you have surpassed them. If you move the throne, you find a passage to the Earth Realm, which is in chaos and the prince there is having trouble keeping the Dark Kingdom Zodiac at bay. He could use all your help. Just look for Andrew Covers in the Earth Realm he will the next guardian to find. My dearest daughter goes with them and bring peace and honor to our family and this realm. It was our duty to protect the Majestic Star Kingdom, and now we can full fill that request. I LOVE YOU FAIZAH." King said.

"I know him. I met him in the Crystal Star of Water and Ice Realm." Sue said.

As Faizah watch her father turn to dust and disappeared. She cried but stood up and looked at the two. Knew that they had to stop this Dark Kingdom Zodiac from causing any more problems for the other realms that are in danger of being overtaken by the Dark Kingdom.

"We need to go. Sue, do you have enough power to get us to the Crystal Star of Earth Realm." Faizah said with tears in her eyes.

"Yes, just help me move the throne so we can get moving." Sue said.

Joey went over and started to move the throne with the help of Faizah they saw a mirror that at one touch from Sue had turned into the light portal, but it was different from her own power, but very familiar to her, it must have been her parents to do this. The portal opened and the three guardians walked through it. As they walked through the portal Sue knew that her beloved parents had their hands on them and protecting them from any more harm while going through the portal. Sue knew that the Dark Kingdom Zodiac could not enter her light portal because of being pure good, but she was not sure about the one her parents had made for them. Something told her that they could not enter this portal either.

The Crystal Star of the Earth Realm

Chapter 16

$\rightarrowtail\!\cdot\!\diamond\!\cdot\!\odot\!\cdot\!\diamond\!\cdot\!\leftarrowtail$

As the three guardians enter the Earth Realm, there seemed to be something hovering in the air. They could feel evil across the land and that it was not going to be an easy task for them. As they started to walk, they heard things breaking beneath their feet. As they looked down, they saw dead plants, animals' bones, and other bones they did not want to know about. As they looked up and notice that they seemed to be in a valley of some kind. Not sure what kind but some kind. As they keep moving it started to make them very uneasy to see so much death in one area than in a lifetime.

"This must be the Valley of Death in this realm." Faizah said.

"You might be onto something. Let us just keep going before night falls upon us." Joey said.

"Agreed. Let us move quickly. Joey, can you summon a dragon to get us out of this valley?" Sue asked.

"I will try, but it might be a dead zone." Joey said laughing.

"Not funny at all. I think some of these bones might be human, like a battle took place here." Faizah said.

"Joey stops with the jokes please. We need to focus on finding Andrew." Sue said.

"Okay. Just wanted to lighten up the mood, that is all." Joey said feeling defeated.

"I'm glad you are trying but now is not the time. I feel a strange energy here and not a good one either." Sue said.

"I summon the Dragon of Wind. Use wind cyclone." Joey called.

As the dragon appeared and landed next to Joey and the girls, the dragon seemed to be on edge. As they climbed up on the dragon's back to fly out of the valley something happened. The earth started to shake, and something started to move and when the guardians turned around it was too late. A huge skeleton was walking near them made up of all kinds of bones as if someone had summoned it. The Wind Dragon let a huge guest of wind out hitting the skeleton and making it shake some so they had time to get out of the valley, but the skeleton was not going to let them leave without being defeated first.

"Lightning come to me. Lightning Bolt Strike." Faizah said.

As the lightning hit the skeleton it turned back into a pile of bones, and they were able to get out of the valley of death. As the Wind Dragon carried them over the valley the three guardians looked around and they saw a land that had seen many battles over the years. It was dry like a dessert; it had cacti, all kinds of other dessert plants, and most likely a lot of dessert animals. While fly overhead they notice a place they can land and set up camp it they need to.

"There is a cliff over there that we can set up camp." Joey said.

"I see it; we can stay there for the night but need to get a move on in the morning. It also has plenty of shade to keep us cool from the dessert heat." Faizah said.

Sue moved up on the dragon to get a better look at what they are looking at and she agreed to. It had already started to get dark as they landed under the cliff and the cool dessert started to get colder. So, they started a fire to keep warm after Joey had released his summons on the Wind Dragon only to call the Light and Travel Dragon to bring them there stuff.

"How is it possible for you to summon a dragon this big and when we were in my castle in the Lightning Realm it was way smaller to bring your weapons?" Faizah said.

"Well, if we need a certain thing from the dragons, they can come in any size to bring us what we need. It is more done with the Light and Travel

Dragon than the others because it can control space around her." Joey said.

"Does she have a name?" Faizah asked.

"She says her name is Petunia." Joey said with a little laugh.

Then the dragon nipped him for laughing at her name. Faizah started to laugh when the dragon looked at her, she stopped.

"She hates her name too, but that is what her mother named her when she was born. She also likes you; she thinks that you are very pretty and funny looking because she has never seen a human like elf before with violet hair color, amber eyes, and a tint of green and purple to your skin." Joey said.

"Oh, way thank you. It is in all the royal family our skin changes color as we get older, my skin may go to a really dark brown with either a green tint to it or a purple tint to it. My family also can live for many centuries before they have children or pass on, unless they are killed like my father was. He was getting ready to turn a thousand years old when the Joker killed him. He was a very young prince and just getting ready to marry my mother when the Majestic Star Kingdom had come under attack. I'm only 18 years old I would be considering a baby in his eyes because I was so young. With the dark kingdom attacking our realm my body became a young woman's body and I started to age at the same rate as you do which means they already had their teeth in my realm, before you both got there.

Also, since the Star Princess is the only one with the power to bring balance back to all the realms then I would stop aging so fast. I have slowed on the aging thing for now, but I think that has a lot to do with the fact the guardians are starting to wake to their true powers." Faizah said.

"I'm sorry for your lost. It is good to know a little bit more about you. I did notice you had pointed ears, your is long and the color of violet, and your skin and eye color were different from the ones' we have met before. I think that having different races in our guardians' is a really good thing." Joey said.

"Yeah, it makes things really interesting to say the least. Also, I think that I would like to get to know more about you and your realm." Sue said.

"I would like that too." Faizah said.

"Petunia said "that you are a very interesting race, and she likes you a lot." Joey told her.

"Well Joey, you think you can release your Light Dragon and get some rest while we girls take first watch." Faizah said.

"Yeah, but she wants to stay and help keep watch as well. She said I don't have to release the summons she will stay as long as I don't need another dragon." Joey said.

"Okay, then she is more than welcome to help keep watch." Faizah said smiling at the dragon.

As Joey went and laid down, he fell asleep quickly because of summoning two dragons in one day, fighting an evil skeleton, and betting the dark general of the Dark Kingdom Zodiac in the last 24 hours. They were all very tired but Faizah and Sue wanted to get to know each other better, and Petunia the Light and Travel Dragon wanted to help the girls out because she likes Sue because of using the light and travel power and being the guardian of the Crystal Star of Light and Travel, and the reason she likes Faizah so much was because she seemed to be very interesting to her, and she didn't want to be released and not get the chance to see her again.

As the girls talked for most of the night, they knew more about each other than any guy they have ever met. They were laughing when Joey woke up and walked over to them and he cleared his throat to let them know he was standing there. The girls looked around and just looked at him and started to laugh even harder.

"What is so funny?" Joey asked.

"Inside joke." Sue said.

"Really, do you mind telling me the joke?" Joey asked.

"Okay, okay your hair is sticking up all over the place and you talk in your sleep. Lola, Lola, Lola please don't go. Hang on I'm coming." Faizah said.

"That is not funny." Joey said getting mad.

"Oh, come on cuz we are just playing around. Did you sleep well, or do you still miss Lola?" Sue said and started to laugh hard.

Joey walked away from the girls and went back to where he was sleeping just to put on his shoes again, and his shirt because it was too hot to wear the clothes to bed. When he looked up his notice that the sun had started to rise, and he realize the girls let him sleep all night long instead of waking him up like they said they would.

"Why didn't either of you two wake me?" Joey asked.

"We felt you needed more sleep because you looked very drain. Also, we lost track of time because of getting to know each other and Petunia has been a really big help, so you own her some time off. She went out and got us some water too cook with from one of the cacti out in the dessert. Are you hungry?" Faizah asked.

"Yeah, I'm starving, what did you make?" Joey asked.

"Lizard and snake eggs." Sue said trying to keep her face straight.

"No thanks, I think I will find me something else to eat." Joey said.

Faizah started to laugh even harder because Sue was giving joey a hard time and they had regular eggs and some sausages with coffee for breakfast which the girls felt they were going to need it.

"Joey it is regular eggs as in chicken eggs, and sausages that you guys had in your ruck sack that Petunia has been carrying for you since you left the Crystal Star of Water and Ice Realm. You also had coffee in there which we needed." Faizah said.

"Okay, will you please stop with joking around I did not sleep well, I'm worried about everyone, and we need to find this Andrew person." Joey said.

"Okay we will stop, please eat something. Andrew, I think you met him before. I met him in the Crystal Star of Water and Ice Realm. As matter of fact, he kissed me, and Leroy caught us." Sue said.

"I did not meet him, but that does explain Leroy acting like he did with you. I was thinking you didn't deserve to be treated or mouth talked, but now I know way he was so mad. You do know he liked you a lot right." Joey said.

"Yeah, I do know he did, but he wanted to be with Alena, and I knew this from the beginning when he asked me out. I'm not mad about it because I also knew that Alena really liked him, and I just stepped in and well you know the rest. I feel bad about that because friends shouldn't do that to each other, but I was jealousy that every time a new guy came to school, they would check her out and wouldn't give me a second look. I know Alena hated that and that she would tell me I was much prettier than her, but she didn't see what they had seen in her." Sue said.

"It happens, look at what happened to Lynn and me all over a guy, but the deference between her and you are that it did not change you, it did make you do other things, but it did not change your heart and loyalty to your best friend." Faizah said.

"Yeah, you are right. Alena forgave me for it, and we are even closer than what we use to be." Sue said with more confidence.

All three friends sat down and ate what little breakfast they had before heading out into the dessert. After packing things up again and giving them to the light dragon they headed out into the dessert where the sun was already high into the sky, and they could feel it getting hotter. So, they would walk over to a cactus and get water from it. As they kept moving finally, they have reached a small dessert town. As they start to go near it the ground starts to shake under them again and this time a dinosaur came out of the ground with just bones and no meat or skin on it. The three guardians didn't know what to do, because it the dessert kill them this thing was going to. Then someone spoke and they looked up and on the back of the dinosaur's neck was man.

"Who are you?" Sue asked.

"Well, I can tell you and your friends are guardians by the power you are putting off. You can call me Marcus. I'm the general of the dead. This is where you will be stopped guardians." Marcus said.

"You can try, but we are not that easily beaten." Faizah said.

"Well then guardian of lightning has a go at my pet. You had trouble beating my skeleton back in the valley of death, this one will be hard to fight." Marcus said.

"I summon the Earth Dragon. Rockslide." Joey called.

"I call the light balls to me. Circle the enemy." Sue said.

"Lightning come to me. Purple Lightning Stream." Faizah said.

As the fight started Marcus disappeared into the dust of the dessert, as the triceratops attacked them. It would drive into the ground only to come up making the ground shake more and more. Sue was able to slow it down by aiming her light powers at it, when Faizah hit it with a thunder bolt this time, and Joey used the Earth Dragon's quake power swallowing the dinosaur up. It had taken many hours to defeat the dinosaur, but they had managed. Marcus had come back and was applauding them.

"Well done guardians you are a lot stronger than I thought you might be. Next it won't be so easy. I also have the prince and guardian of this realm in my custody. So come the Earth Realm's castle which looks like an Egyptian Castle in the far-off distances. Just this guardian I will not make it easy for you to get there." Marcus said.

Chapter 17

The guardians finished with Marcus and went into the dessert town to discover that there is an oasis located in the back of town. They walked to the inn to get rooms to sleep and rest because they knew that they had a long way ahead of them before they could find Andrew and the castle which Marcus had mention to them. As they walked into the inn, the inn keeper looked up and gave an ugly face as if he was tired of dealing with tourist coming and going.

"Excuse me sir can we have three room please." Faizah asked.

"If you pay, I think I might have three room open." Inn Keeper said.

"Do you or don't you have three rooms." Faizah asked.

"I have two rooms opened, one with a single bed and the other with two beds. Will that work?" Inn Keeper said.

"Yes, that will be fine. How much are the rooms?" Faizah asked.

"$50 per night each room in gold only. How long will you be staying?" Inn Keeper asked.

"Three nights and two days." Faizah said.

"Okay that will be $300 dollars in gold for three nights and two days for both rooms." Inn Keeper said.

"Okay, here is the $300 in gold for both rooms." Faizah said.

As Faizah pulls out the money Sue notice that the money had changed from regular money to gold from the Lightning Realm to the Earth Realm. Joey took out what little money he had on him and saw that it had changed to. He also pulled out his credit card and saw that it had changed too. Which means every time they change realms, they are given what they need for that realm if they have it on them. As they put everything back into their pockets and go to their rooms and dropped off there things, they headed down to the oasis to eat and order food they saw children playing in the water to stay cool. The town was not so bad with the dessert just outside their front door, there seemed to be a nice cool breeze coming into the town just enough to keep them cool as if someone was looking out for them. Also entering the town of Oasis through the dessert was also the only way in and out of the town. It was very beautiful the town it had a small beach, palm trees, some trees with bananas on them, coconuts, mangos, and people laughing an enjoying life as if nothing seemed to be wrong. Oasis was a peaceful town and the guardians' wanted to keep it that way. As they sit and watch the children play, parents spending time with family and friends, and them eating. The food was so good that they had seconds, they even tried coconut juice which was very sweet, and they loved it.

"This place is so peaceful; I hope that we can keep it that way." Sue said.

"Yeah, it is like stepping into a movie and everything is as good as heaven." Joey said.

"I think that we can stay here in this spot for a little bit longer, but we still need to find the guardian of earth to keep this peace." Faizah said.

"We agree with you." Sue and Joey said together.

As it started to get even darker the guardians headed back to the inn to get some sleep and hopeful look around town for some answer on how to find the castle of this realm. Sue and Faizah went to their room while Joey went to his room. The girls shared a room because it had two beds instead of one and it might look off if one guy had two women in his bed with him even though it was not like that.

As the girls enter their room, they notice there was a window, and it was opened to let in the breeze from the dessert and smell from the water. It smells like an ocean, that was salt water, the breeze was very much welcomed by the girls. The room has two standard size beds, one window, it was paneling on the wall with some design on it that matched the town. The beds had head broads that looked like bamboo sticks, and the sheets where light in weight and very comfortable with colors of red and white. The floor is made up of wood and shines as if polished everyday by the workers. The inn felt more like home then staying in a hotel. The bathroom was small, but it had a nice shower and tub to take baths in. Sue had taken the bed on the left near the window, and Faizah took the bed on the right. It was good to be able to sleep in a regular bed since they had left the Lightning Realm. Sue feels a sleep rather fast, the minute her head it the pillow, and Faizah could not go to sleep right away so she stayed up thinking before falling into an uneasy sleep. She dreamed she was in the Majestic Star Kingdom; it was so beautiful that she could not believe anyone would want to destroy this magic place. She felt the warmth of friends, family, and peace. She looked over and there standing was a man she realized was her father at a very young age and in his arms was a woman so beautiful that she made the flowers stand out. It was her mother; they were in a garden and dancing by the looks of things. As she looked down at her own self she was where a dress made up of light slick and lace in the color of purple and white. She turned in the dress just to see it shine, and the lace flowed like air. The main part of the dress went to her knees, and the lace came down then opened in front like curtain does on a window. It was so beautiful that she must be at a dance of some kind. Then see looked around and notice that there were others there too. They all stopped dancing when they heard trumpets blow to announce the Queen, King, and Star Princess. She looked up and she saw the Star Princess in a beautiful grown as well.

"We would like to thank all of you for coming to the Star Princess' 16th birthday party. As honored guess new and old friends, new and old guardians. Thank you for your help as always." The King said.

Then after the announcement she lost the dream because someone was waking her up. As she starts to wake up, she sees Sue shaking her. Faizah sat up straight up on the bed roll that is her sleeping bag so she can see what was going on.

"Faizah time to get up, breakfast is here, and so is Joey. We need to get information about Andrew and the castle." Sue said.

"Sue, way is you waking me up, I was having this most wonderful dream about the Majestic Star Kingdom and the Star Princess." Faizah said.

"I'm sorry but you did ask for a wakeup call and we got it. Not only that we all have had some type of dream about the Majestic Star Kingdom and the Star Princess, but we never get to see her face ever." Sue said.

"You have had this dream before?" Faizah asked.

"Yes, mine was at a ball in a grand ballroom." Sue replied.

"Mine was in a garden outside with a balcony overlooking the garden with the Queen, King, and Star Princess." Faizah said.

"That sounds about right." Sue and Joey said.

As soon as Joey had spoken Faizah jumped from the bed and ran to the bathroom to get dress.

"Sue you could have told me he was in our room." Faizah said.

"I did but you weren't listening." Sue said screaming through the door.

"Sorry. I should have waited to come in." Joey said.

"It is okay it happens." Faizah said coming out of the bathroom.

The Inn Keeper had brought them some clothes to wear because the clothes they had been too heavy for the dessert. So, they ate and went out into the town and started to ask people at the café if they have heard of a castle in the dessert. As they had spoken to many people until they found someone to help them.

"Excuse me mam?" Joey said.

"Yes, young man?" Old Woman said.

"I was wondering if you might have heard of a castle in the dessert." Joey said.

"Oh, yes I have it belongs to the royal family. Why are you looking for the castle?" Old woman said.

"We are looking for our friend who happens to be in some kind of trouble." Joey said.

"Well, it is a few days ride from here if you ride a camel." Old Woman said.

"Oh, that is great, which direction is the castle in from here?" Sue asked.

"It is to the West of this town. There is another town just before you reach the castle and it is called Grovetown, once you reached that town the castle is only maybe a few miles away. In Grovetown you will need written permission to enter as well as being a merchant that is selling something." Old Woman said.

"How can we get permission? Who do we speak too?" Joey asked.

"Here I was told to give this to people who might be looking for the castle of the dessert. It will let you enter the town and sell goods." Old Woman said.

"Thank you so very much." Sue said.

As the friends compute the information, they got from the old woman they started making plans for how they are going to get there. For the next two days they had decided for camels to take them though the dessert, they only would stop long enough to eat, and rest. They also had brought a lot of fabric just in case the town they were sent to be a trade town. As they stopped on their last day in the dessert, they choose to rest under the dessert stars, and something seemed to make the camels very uneasy. As the guardians looked around, they seen a saber tooth tiger approach them and it was starting to get bigger and bigger the closer it got. As it was near them it no longer had any fur or meat on it, it was only bone. As the tiger pounced at them. They ran out of the way only to have another trigger come from behind them and before they knew they had been surrounding by at six saber tooth tigers. So, Faizah had called fourth her powers and many lightning strikes hit at once taking out the saber tooth tigers. Faizah had passed out from using her powers at that strength which made it hard for them to keep going because they were all tired from their travel. So good thing they choose to rest that night in the open because there was no cover from the dessert.

As they had made a trip that would take any other traveler longer than it took them to get to the town. As they approached the town someone had come to the entrance and stopped them from entering.

"May we pass please?" Faizah said.

"What business do you have in a trade town?" Guard asked.

"We are selling fabric for a brand-new company called the Guardians' Fabric." Sue said.

"Have you got permission to sell your goods here?" Guard said.

"Yes, we have sir. Prince Andrew gave us permission to sell our goods." Faizah said.

As Faizah handed over the written note the Old Woman had given them in Oasis Town just before leaving. The Guard took the letter and read it as he looked over it many times to make sure that is was not fake, he gave it back to them.

"You may enter but watch yourselves I will be keeping an eye on you three." Guard said.

"Thank you, sir." Sue said.

"Hold up, why is there a man selling fabrics with two very lovely women?" Guard asked stepping back in their way because he did not notice Joey at first.

"Sir I'm there older brother, and their bodyguard just in case they got attacked on their way here. I will also be helping them with their business." Joey said.

"Okay, go right on in." Guard said.

The three guardians enter the town and set up their merchant tent just a little way into the town. When they looked around, they notice a lot of merchants setting up tents. Sue walked over to one of the tents and started to look around at what they had.

"Hello, miss how can I help you today?" Merchant One asked.

"Yes, how much is that necklace, and why are there so many merchants in town today?" Sue asked.

"The necklace is $550 in gold, and there is a festival coming to town tonight." Merchant One said.

"Oh, thank you very much. I will have to come back and check on that necklace." Sue said walking away.

"Okay misses have a nice day." Merchant One said.

As Sue returned to their tent, she informed Faizah and Joey about the festival going on tonight. The reason there is some many guards at each entrance to the town.

Chapter 18

As Sue was telling them about the festival that was going on that night and that they needed to get a room at the inn in this town before they are all filled up. So, Faizah went looking for an inn and booking at least two rooms if able too. As Faizah is looking around town, she felt weak from the other night. She needed rest, but before she could rest, they needed a room to rest in. As she walks by this pub, she hears people in the pub talking about some strange things going on in the dessert. The only thing that would make strange is the fact that the Dark Kingdom Zodiac was behind all the strange things in the dessert. As she walks in the pub she goes to the bar.

"What can I get for you miss?" Bar Tender asked.

"Well seeing as I'm on break can I get a Root beer please?" Faizah said.

"Yes, would like anything else?" Bar Tender asked.

"No, just the root beer for now. If you don't mind, I would like to seat here and drink since it is a little cooler in here than outside." Faizah said.

"That is fine miss." Bar Tender replied.

Faizah sat at the bar listening to the two men talk about what was going on and how the earth seemed to be dying because the royal family is hurting. The King had lost his life last year, the Queen passed a few months ago, and the prince happens to be missing. As the men talk way into the night Joey and Sue came looking for Faizah and when they entered the pub, she was at the bar sitting.

"Hey, Faizah what have you been doing all this time?" Sue asked.

"What, Oh Sue and Joey it is you. I'm sorry I lost track of time." Faizah said.

"It is okay we all do that. Did you find us a place to sleep for at tonight?" Joey asked.

"No, I got caught up in listening to these two men talking about strange things happening in the dessert." Faizah said.

"It sounds like the Dark Kingdom Zodiac is at it again." Sue said.

"Yeah, it does, and worst is that it is affecting the people around the area." Faizah said.

"We'll let us get something to eat and drink then find a place for the night." Joey suggested.

"Good idea." Sue said.

"Bar Tender can we get three rounds of Root Beer and maybe a pizza?" Joey asked.

"I can give you the root beers, but all we serve is sandwiches here. Would like a sandwich sir?" Bar Tender asked.

"Yes, one turkey sub, chicken beast sub, and a roast beef sub, three rounds of root beer please, also if we can have a table that would be great too." Joey said.

"Okay three subs coming up, along with three root beers, and you three can have that table in the corner over there." Bar Tender said.

As the three guardians walked over to the table in the corner of the pub while waiting on their food and drinks to come, they started to talk about what the two men had talked about early that day when Faizah told them what she overheard. She had been at the pub for a good five hours and just listened to what people were saying, but what got her attention was those two men.

"You see that we need to get a move on, and we can't stay here any longer than two days at the most." Faizah said.

"You are right, if we want to avoid this realm going into chaos like the others have when the Dark Kingdom has been involved." Sue said.

As they continued to talk about what to do next the waitress came over with their food and drinks and left them alone to talk. As she walked away Joey had stopped her and she turned back around to look at him when he had to ask her something.

"Excuse me miss, is there any inns around here that is not full yet?" Joey asked.

"Well, sir you can stay here we do have rooms open, they are not much like the other inns, but those inns are already filled up and booked solid because of the festival and the merchants that has come from all across the land to this year's festival." Waitress said.

"How much are your rooms?" Joey asked.

"Let me get the bar tender and he can answer that question for you." Waitress said.

As the waitress went to get the bar tender so they can get an answer to their question. The bar tender came over to their table to let them know the prince of the rooms he does have open which isn't much.

"The rooms are $75 per night in gold." Bar Tender said.

"Okay, how many rooms do you have open?" Joey asked.

"I only have one left. Will you be taking that one room?" Bar Tender said.

"Yes, we will take that room sir." Joey said.

"Then how many nights and days will you be staying?" Bar Tender asked.

"We will be staying two nights and two days." Joey said.

"Then the price will be $150 for both nights and days." Bar Tender said.

"Okay here is the money please could you wake us up around 7:30 am so that we can open our shop." Joey asked.

"Yes." Bar Tender said.

The three guardians stayed up late that night talking after they had went to their room when the pub was closing. Faizah had gone to sleep a little after they went to their room, because she was tired and that she knew that she needed her rest. Joey and Sue understood all too well because each guardian has either passed out after using their powers when they first receive them, or they can go for days before it could happen to where they needed to use all their might to stop an attack. So, when Faizah went to bed Joey and Sue was surprised that she had not passed out before had when she used her powers the night before, which met that she had some strong stemma to keep going until she finally passed out that night.

The next morning, they got the wakeup call, but instead up waking up Faizah they let her sleep and Joey and Sue went to their shop to open. They n=knew that Faizah would join them later after she woke and ate something. A few hours went by, and Faizah started to wake. When she finally woke up all the way she notices that Joey and Sue were gone.

"Please let them be okay." Faizah said out loud.

As she went down to the bar she talked to the waitress from the night before and she told her that the bar tender needed to talk to her. As Faizah walked over to the bar she sat down on a stool and the Bar Tender came over to her gave her some coffee, and banana nut muffins for breakfast and a note. The note was from Sue telling Faizah they were at the shop and didn't want to wake her. So, she hurried up and finished her breakfast and paid the bar tender and went down to the shop.

As she reached the shop there was a lot of people standing around looking at the fabric they had and some of the fabric had been brought which was good for them because this would give them more money to help with finding the guardian of the Crystal Star of the Earth Realm.

"Hey, do you guys want some help?" Faizah asked.

"Yeah, you can start by ringing everyone up that is ready to pay while Joey cuts and I assist the customers." Sue said.

As Faizah did as she asked, she felt good just to have friends like these two. As the first customer paid for their fabric and left the others did too, and about around 4pm it started to slow because the festival was starting so it meet it was time to close shop. As they head to the pub to eat, get something to drink, and clean up and change their clothes into something a little better suited for the festival. They left the pub and went down to the festival to enjoy it. It was not like any festival they have every been too. It had all kinds of food places, games, and some entertainment going on. Which was good considering this was their last night at the pub and knew they had to get a move on to find Andrew to set things right and knowing he is the guardian of this realm as well. As they watch on with joy at the festival, they run into someone by accident.

"Oh, I'm so sorry." Sue said.

"It is alright my dear." Old Woman said.

"It is you!" Sue said.

"Oh, how nice it is to see you again young lady. I see you were able to get into town without a problem." Old Woman said.

"Yeah, we did have just a little bit of trouble, but not much." Sue said.

"Oh, good. By the way my name is Ruth Kite." Ruth said.

"It is nice to meet you Ruth, my name is Sue Stang; this here is Joseph Ryan, and Faizah Carter." Sue said.

"Well, it was nice to finally get your names guardians'." Ruth said.

"WHAT! How did you know we are guardians?" Faizah asked.

"Well, you see my grandson is the prince of this realm, and its most powerful guardian. His name is Andrew Kites." Ruth said.

"You are the Queen of this realm?" Sue asked.

"No, my dear, I had passed my crown down to my daughter-in-law and my son. Who bared a healthy baby boy 20 years ago." Ruth said.

"Oh, I'm sorry. I met Andrew once in the Crystal Star of Water and Ice Realm." Sue said.

"I know young lady he told me. Also, I know that you are here to help us out, which means I will be taking up my former duty as Queen until he can return from finding the Star Princess. Also please keep it low that I'm here, I have been in hiding since my grandson protected me from the Dark Kingdom Zodiac." Ruth said.

"We will do are best to help find him." Joey said.

"I thank you very many guardians. Now please enjoy the festival tonight because it may not be this peaceful again for a long time." Ruth said.

As the guardians enjoyed the festival way into the night. They are here a loud bang and then seen something coming their way and all the peoples' way as the guards are running into the town, they notice that something was chasing them. As it was coming closer, they notice that it was a monster. As the guardians come together in a line to stop the monster from going any further it just disappeared as if it was never there. Then they heard a very loud yell behind them and standing there was the monster holding Ruth with its tongue and it was a giant lizard of nothing but bones. They knew that the general Marcus was behind this, and he was going to stop the guardians at all costs.

As Sue runs to help Ruth the giant Lizard pins her down with a foot and starts to pull Ruth into its' mouth. Faizah uses her powers over lightning to try and stop the giant lizard from eating Ruth.

"Lightning Bolt strike that giant lizard." Faizah called.

As the lightning bolt hit the giant lizard it became dazed and dropped Ruth to the guard and Sue was free from its foot.

"Light Ring bind that giant lizard." Sue called.

As the light rings bind the lizard and it started to struggle against its' bindings the light rings only got tighter. Then Joey steps up and was getting ready to summon the Earth Dragon when the ground started to shake again and as they turned around there was a lot of giant bone lizards coming after the towns' people to be eaten.

"Faizah we are going to need multiply strikes of lightning to slow those giant lizards down or turn them to dust. Sue, you think you can send out a lot of light rings to bind them all. While I summon the Earth Dragon." Joey said.

"Yeah, I think I can do that." Sue said.

Faizah seemed to be scared to do this because she was a farad that if she used all that power again, she might pass out on her friends when they need her the most.

"Faizah, can you do It.?" Joey asked her again.

"Faizah, I know you are scared but you have better control over your powers now then what you did two days ago." Sue said.

With Sue's positive thinking, Faizah knew she could do it this time, she knew that it might drain but not as much as it did the first time, she used that power.

"Yes, I can do it." Faizah said.

"That is the spirit." Sue said.

"Thanks for having trust in me." Faizah said.

"Don't mention it and we can do the girly thing later right now we have worked to do." Sue said.

"Right!" Faizah said.

As the three guardians' get ready to use their powers at their fullest and was going to protect those in this town from all these monsters and what has been happening in the dessert, they needed to find Andrew and soon. If not and they are too late this realm would be doomed for good. Then the Dark Kingdom Zodiac would have even more hold on all the realms if they could not save this one from them, so they were not going to let that happen in this time or any other time. They have suffered enough at the Dark Kingdom Zodiac's hands when they destroyed the Majestic Star Kingdom and took their beloved star princess away from them. So, the guardians were going to let them have it.

"Light rings come fourth and bind all those giant bone lizards." Sue called.

"Lightning Strom come and turn those giant bone lizards into dust." Faizah called. "I summon the Earth Dragon let those giant lizards be barred again and forever." Joey called.

As the powers came and hit every one of the giant bone lizards to save the people of this town.

All the light rings Sue sent out bind all the giant bone lizards, the lightning storm had turned all the giant bone lizards to dust, and while the earth dragon used quake to barrier all the giant bone lizards' dust forever. The three guardians fell to their knees breathing heavy from all the power they had used to save everybody in town. As they are graining their breath back after the fight with the giant bone lizards they turn and see that the town's people are all okay, and so is Ruth, and them.

Chapter 19

All the towns' people chaired the guardians on for getting rid of the giant bone lizards and protecting them. The guardians stood up and turned around waving at the people and thanking them. Every person in town wanted to shake their hands for a job well done, but the guardians knew the job was far from being done, but the people did not need to know this. As the guardians and Ruth walked back to the pub to go to sleep the bar tender met them at the door.

"May we pass please?" Faizah asked.

"You may not pass. I would like that you leave here now." Bar Tender said.

"Why?" Joey asked.

"I don't want any trouble; ever since you three got here we have had nothing but trouble." Bar Tender said.

"What do you mean that "ever since we got here; you have nothing but trouble?"" Sue asked.

"You heard me. He is your money back and your things. So please leave. The towns people might be happy with you right now but come tomorrow they will be blaming you all for what happened here tonight." Bar Tender said.

"Then the people will have to learn the truth." Ruth said

As she stepped forward the bar tender looked at her and his mouth fell, and he knew that she was the Queen of the Crystal Star of the Earth Realm. As she went closer to the bar tender, he started to back away.

"Your highness I did not know you were in town tonight." Bar Tender said.

"Why would I not be it is the festival of the royal family being celebrated tonight, or I'm I wrong?" Ruth asked.

"No, your highness. It has always been about the royal family and how well you treat your people. I'm sorry for being so rude. I will let them in and you, I also will let them stay for free tonight." Bar Tender said.

"That would be great, but they will not be staying here tonight, but we could use a table for a minute." Ruth said.

"Yes mam, will you be staying the night?" Bar Tender asked.

"Yes, I will take their room they are staying in. Okay." Ruth asked.

"That will be fine your highness." Bar Tender said.

As the guardians and Ruth walked into the pub, they take a table and sat down. As they sat the bar tender brought them whatever they wanted to drink, eat, or clothes without charging them because he knew if he showed them kindness the Queen would pay him well for his services. The bar tender was their personal waiter for the night while the Queen informed the guardians that the bar tender is right that they did need to get a move on to the castle to save her grandson from the Dark Kingdom Zodiac's hands.

"How are we supposed to get there?" Sue asked.

"You can ride the camels you rode on coming here." Ruth said.

"We will need supplies for the trip to the castle as well." Joey said.

"I believe the bar tender will be able to help you out." Ruth said.

"How are we going to be able to get into the castle without Marcus finding us?" Faizah asked.

"There is a secret door to the side of the castle that can be used, because that is the same entrance that was used to get me out and from the dark kingdom." Ruth said.

"Well, we have a plan at least." Joey said.

"Yes." Sue and Faizah said together.

"Guardians' please be careful; you are the last hope for this realm and all realms. Until the Star

Princess is be found you are to uphold the peace in her place for now." Ruth said.

"We understand." All Three Guardians said together.

As the bar tender gave them their last supplies the guardians where on their way to the castle which they had been told it should only take them a few hours to get there if they don't stop. So, the guardians agreed to keep moving as much as they could before they must stop and rest. As they went through the dessert they had be traveling for many hours before they had to stopped and rest. As they stop at a huge cactus for shade and water they needed to eat before going on. They were not going to sleep this night or the next night until they have gotten so close to eh castle that is when they will sleep and take up guard for enemies that might come their way. As the cool night air bellowed though the dessert it seemed as if it was comforting them. As they ate sandwiches for dinner that the bar tender gave them along with some drinks, and chips to hold them over until they finished their mission.

"Joey, do you think that we will be able to find the Star Princess and restore peace to all the realms?" Faizah asked.

"I think that if we work together as a team and not against each other than yes we will be able to find her. Also, as long as we trust in each other there is nothing that we can't do." Joey said.

"I agree with Joey, we do need to trust each other and get back to the Crystal Star of Water and Ice with all the guardians and start looking for the Star Princess." Sue said.

"Thanks, you two. That makes me feel better already." Faizah said.

As the guardians finished up their food and started back on their path to the castle to only be stopped by something huge in their way. As the guardians get closer, they see something move and then it really moved. It was a rock rhino that was so big it could take out a New York skyscraper. As it turned, they heard something in their mind.

"Why do you come here?" Rhino asked.

"We come here to save the prince and guardian of this realm." Joey was thinking.

"How do you plan on doing that if you have no weapons, or powers." Rhino asked.

"We have weapons, and we are the guardians of Summoning, Light and Travel, and Lightning." Joey answered.

"Prove to me that you are worth of passing through my domain?" Rhino said.

"Then you are on." Joey said.

As the guardians' got off the camels and tied they to a cactus to keep them from running off and they are forced to walk the rest of the castle. They start to call fourth their powers when the rhino spoke again in their minds.

"No, you attack one at a time and if any of you can beat me, I will let all three passes." Rhino said.

"I will go first." Joey said.

"Go for its Guardian of Summoning." Rhino said.

"I summon the lightning dragon." Joey called.

As the lightning dragon appeared and let out its' attack it barely made any damage to the rhino and then it tried another attack only to be knocked out of the air. Sue stepped up and called fourth her powers of light.

"Guardian of Light gives a try if you think you have what it takes." Rhino said.

"Light balls come to me." Sue called

As the light balls hit the rhino, they did not do much damage either. When Faizah was watching this, and it hit that even through the rhino wanted them to attack on their own she knew it had another meaning to it. As she thought about it then it came to her what Joey had said a little while that they had to work together and trust each to make it through all of this.

"Sue and Joey stop. We need to attack all at once by combining our powers together as a team. Joey, you said, "I think that if we work together as a team and not against each other than yes we will be able to find her." Remember." Faizah said.

"You are right we need to work as a team to get through this test." Joey said.

"Then let us attack together." Sue said.

"You got it." Joey and Faizah said together.

"Lightning Bolt come to me." Faizah called.

"Light rings come to me." Sue called.

"Lightning Dragon I call you to use thunder bolt." Joey called.

As all three powers combined and hit the rhino, it had made so much damage that they heard the rhino in their minds again and this time it was not for testing them but congratulating them for a well learned teamwork.

"Guardians' you have done well, no one has ever been able to bet like you have this night. You may pass through my domain and reach the castle on the other side which is only a mile long from this spot. Again, well done, you have passed the test. Good Luck." Rhino said.

"Thank you for showing us what teamwork can do." Faizah said.

As the rhino had disappeared into the night and opened a path for the guardians to follow so they could make it to the castle before night was over. They got back on the camels and headed in the dictation the rhino had pointed them so they can get there and save the guardian of earth and the prince of this realm. As the three guardians continue their way they had been smiling after their victory against the rhino and ruler of this domain, that there is a chance that all the guardians' will be able to have a good teamwork with each other.

As night started to turn into day, they notice they have traveled all night from the town to the castle, but when they looked up it was not like any castle, they have ever seen it had a shape of a pyramid as a roof top, some pillars are white, with heads of animals on the corners of the roof all made up of gold. As they approached the castle to enter, they were stopped by a barrier that would not let them pass.

"What did Ruth say we had to do to get inside?" Sue asked.

"We need to go in on the side and that we will know that side." Faizah said.

"Which means; that side would be weaker than the rest of the barrier." Joey said.

The three guardians started to touch the sides to see where the barrier might be weaker so they could get inside of the castle and save Andrew from the Dark Kingdom Zodiac and hoping that he will help them find the Star Princess and the rest of the guardians. As they look for the weakness in the barrier they walk around it until Sue damn falls through the barrier, she yells for the other two guardians, and they come running as she shows them the part that just opened to her touch, they notice a door there. Sue kept her hand on the barrier while the other two walked in first then she walked in the barrier as she did the barrier became whole once more. They walk over to the door and when Faizah touches it, the door just opened as if it was waiting on them to get there. All three guardians walk in the door to find themselves in a cellar with all kinds of bottles and food being stored there. They look around to find that there is a set of stairs that lend up to a hall that might go on forever, but they had to take the chance that this was the only way to find the guardian and prince of this realm. Also, to stop Marcus from causing any more trouble for the Earth Realm.

The guardians go up the stairs to find that there was not a hall at all but a kitchen full of maids preparing food and drinks for the castle. As the maids turn to see who just came up from the cellar, they notice that these people were not a part of the castle severs or workers. As the maids start scramble to find some things to stop the guardians with Sue spoke up with her hands held in front of her to show that they don't mean no harm.

"Please ladies come down we are not here to hurt you. We came on the Queen's orders and to save Prince Andrews." Sue said.

"Let me get this straight you want us to trust you when you broke into our home, and say you are here on the Queen's orders to help Prince Andrew." Marilyn said.

"Yes, we are not like Marcus who is got the prince locked up here most likely in a cage." Sue said.

"We know he is, but Marcus told us if we disobey him that the prince would be killed and so will the Queen. He has already taken the King which was Prince Andrew's grandfather because his parents died at a young age after he was born." Marilyn said.

"We know, Ruth told us. Let us help, we can save him just give us some server clothes and let us take the food to Marcus." Sue said.

"You want us to help you, and how do you know the Queen's first name?" Marilyn said.

"She told it to us when we were in Grovetown during the festival." Joey said.

As Joey spoke the girls jumped because they did not see him at first and Sue had forgotten that Faizah and Joey were with her for a spit second.

"Oh, my you are good looking." Marilyn said.

"Um, thanks. Please help us we can set you all free just let us help you out by helping us out." Joey pleaded with Marilyn.

"Fine we will lend you some server clothes to get into the throne room, it is almost lunch time and he is going to be wondering where his lunch is soon, but for the girls I'm a feared they are going to have to be entertainment for Marcus because he always has belly dancers at his meal times and the two that was supposed to be her quit last night because all he wanted to do was touch them and they did not like that. For you sir you can be the server and the girls the belly dancers." Marilyn said.

"Okay we will do it. Thanks very much. My name is Sue, this here is Faizah, and the so handsome guy over here my cousin Joey." Sue said.

"Well, it is nice to meet you three. My name is Marilyn and I'm the head maid here. These are my girls." Marilyn said.

"It is nice to meet you all as well." Faizah said.

As they start to get dress the server outfit was a European style outfit for a man, and the belly dancer outfits, one is blue, purple, and yellow in a half tank top, with pants style which Faizah put on which went well with her complication, and the other belly dancer outfit was a skirt type style with a swimsuit top in the colors of pink, green, and orange color which Sue put on which also went well with her complication. The girls looked in the mirror that was providing for them. They left their hair down with a vial over their face and hair only showing their eyes of Blue and Amber so that Marcus could not recognize them.

Chapter 20

They gather up the food on trays to take to the throne room for Marcus, the guardians needed time to get ready for a big fight that was coming their way. As the three guardians' take out the food to the throne room to provide Marcus's food and entertainment.

Joey enters the throne from the server quarters and the girls will enter from the front, then will start dancing to whatever music they have to play for the belly dance just to keep Marcus focus on them so he will not see Joey's face. As Joey takes the food over by the tables where he will put the food down and start to server Marcus the doors open and a song started to play called "Belly Dancer" By Akon when the girls enter the room and was dancing. Marcus had the biggest smile on his face when he saw the girls and forgot all about the food that was being handed to him by Joey. He gets up from the throne and walks near the girls and started to touch them as Marilyn said he does while Andrew was in the cage made up of bone Joey walks over to the throne and he notice a sword which had a gold handle, and the blade was made up of diamond dust. As Joey approached the cage Andrew was too busy watching the girls but most of all her was watching the girl who had light cycling her while she turns instead of the girl who had lightning coming around her as she danced, but Marcus didn't think anything of it. He liked that they were using devise to make light and lightning cycle them because every time he tried to touch the girls the light would cycle one girl and the lightning would cycle the other girl. The throne room was very net it had pillows on the floor in all colors, a throne which was a chair made up of gold and silver, and there are curtains that are made up of different types of color and design like European.

Joey approached the cage while Marcus was focus on the girls and trying to touch them when he saw Andrew's face, he was getting mad and started to shake the cage, but Marcus could not hear him over the music because it was so loud so that Joey can get the prince out.

"Excuse me prince?" Joey said making Andrew jump and turn around.

"Who are you?" Andrew asked.

"I'm Joseph Ryan guardian of the Crystal Star of Summoning." Joey said.

"It is nice to meet you Joseph Ryan, how do you know who I am?" Andrew asked.

"Please just call me Joey, and your grandmother told us who you are." Joey said.

"US? How many are there of you?" Andrew asked.

"The two girls that are dancing and keeping Marcus busy while I try and get you out are also guardians." Joey said.

"I know the one girl I can never forget those blue eyes she has. I want Marcus away from her now." Andrew said.

"She is doing this to get you out of here and safe." Joey said.

"I don't care about that, or would you rather be with her?" Andrew said with anger.

"Um, no she happens to be my cousin, and a guardian." Joey said.

"I know who she is, and I also know if he finds out then there is a good chance, he just might kill her, and I can't bare that if something happens to her. Also, you can't break this cage I have already tried with my powers, the only way to get me out and keep her safe is by betting Marcus." Andrew said.

"Then that is what we will do." Joey said standing up.

As the music stopped Marcus stop trying to touch the girls and went back to the throne. He sat down and looked at the girls and he wanted them to come closer. He was going to choose which girl he was taking to bed with him that night and wanting them to return.

"Please remove your vials." Marcus said.

As the girls looked at each very nervously, they started to take off the vials when Joey came running to them to stop them from doing it. As here reached them they had stopped halfway taking off the vials and the girls looked at him wondering why he had not got Andrew out of the cage.

"What is the meaning of this servant?" Marcus said.

"First I'm no servant of yours, and second to free the prince and guardian of this realm, we need to bet you." Joey said turning around.

Marcus was shocked to see it was him the guardian of summoning. As Joey had reveled who he was the girls finished removing the vials from their faces and Marcus was very pissed off. All three guardians had made it to the castle, not only that they made it in the castle as well. Andrew month fell when Sue had showed her face and he started to shake the cage even harder trying to get out to get near her. There was no luck of doing this.

"SUE RUN FOR IT!!!!! Andrew screamed at her.

As everyone turned to Andrew, Marcus started laughing at the prince. "She will never make it no matter how fast she is. This will be the end for your lover Prince Andrew." Marcus laughed even harder. Sue refuse to leave or even run from this place without at least trying to help.

"I'm not going to run I'm a guardian and I'm not weak. Light Energy Rope. Trap Marcus." Sue said.

The rope missed Marcus by a few inches, but it still made an impact.

"Ah, so she is the one you have been trying to keep away from here. Using your powers over the land and asking certain ancient animals to stop them, on top of me trying to kill them you were trying to save her. It looks as if you failed, and she came on her own free will along with the other two guardians." Marcus said.

"You are nothing but evil, you could never understand what true love is or how it can change your life from a mistake you were going to make." Andrew said.

"Oh, that is right you were to marry the one maid who has some noble blood in her veins." Marcus said laughing.

"Sorry Andrew, but I cannot run away anymore; this is my destiny and I'm going to bare it one way or another along with my friends, and you." Sue said to Andrew.

"PLEASE I BEG YOU TO JUST GET OUT OF HERE SUE!!!! Andrew said while he started to cry.

"I can't." Sue said.

"Please I LOVE YOU WITH ALL MY HEART, and I don't want anything bad to happen to you." Andrew pleaded.

"Sorry, but I AM THE GUARDIAN OF LIGHT AND TRAVEL." Sue yelled it at Andrew.

"Please, like you have a chance against me any of you." Marcus said getting mad.

"Then try us and see how far you can go." Faizah said.

"Enough talk, let's get started." Marcus said.

"Fine." Sue said.

As Marcus grabs his sword another bone animal came up from the ground. This time it was a snake the size of a building. As the snake came near them Sue was the first to step up and use her powers on the snake.

"Light come to me. Light rings bind the snake." Sue said.

"Lightning come to me. Lightning Bolt." Faizah called.

"I summon the lightning dragon. Thunder Bolt." Joey called.

As all the powers hit the snake it had turned to dust and Marcus was so mad now that he attacked the guardians on his own with his sword. As he attacked, he went after Sue first so Andrew could see how much power the Dark Kingdom Zodiac really had and maybe he will surrender to the Dark Kingdom.

"NO!!!" Andrew yelled.

As Marcus tried to get Sue, Faizah had knocked her out of the way taking the hit herself instead of Sue. Faizah only had a scratch on her one leg which also cut the clothes she was wearing. Faizah stood up along with Sue who was unharmed, and Faizah was thankful for.

"Are you okay Sue." Faizah asked.

"Yeah, thanks to you. Now let us get rid of him for good." Sue said.

"I can't agree more." Faizah and Joey said together.

As Marcus attacked again this time all the guardians' jumped out of the way Andrew started to drop to his knees when Marcus raised the sword to attack again.

"Andrew what is wrong with you." Sue called.

"His sword drains my powers every time he attacks or calls his pets to do his bidding." Andrew yelled back.

"That is right and the more I fight you the more he gets weaker." Marcus said laughing.

"You will pay for that." Sue said with anger.

"Now my dear guardian of Light and travel there is no need for that, because you will be dead soon, you have not seen my true powers yet." Marcus said.

"Then let us have it then." Faizah said.

"You don't want that guardian of lightning." Andrew said.

"ENOUGH YOU THREE GUARDAINS' ARE DONE FOR!!!! Marcus yelled at them.

"COME ON!!!! Joey yelled back.

"DARK EARTH POWER COME TO ME. QUAKE! Marcus called.

As the earth beneath the guardians' feet started to shake and open to sallow the three guardians made them all fall onto the ground and started to sink. As this was happen Sue was the first one to be almost pulled in pissing off Andrew so bad that his powers seemed to return to him.

"I CALL EARTH TO ME!!!!! QUICKSAND SALLOW MARCUS UP!!!! Andrew called.

As the quicksand had done as Andrew asked of it; Marcus had disappeared in the quicksand saving all the guardians and leaving the diamond sword behind. The cage holding Andrew crumbled to the ground letting Andrew out. He rushed over to Sue and held her so close that she could not breath.

"Andrew please let me go, I'm fine." Sue said.

"Don't ever do that again." Andrew said.

"I am sorry, but it can't be avoided I'm a guardian and I know you want to protect me from harm but sometimes we have to do things we don't want to do." Sue said.

"Still, you scared me there for a minute." Andrew said.

As Andrew let Sue go, he was helping her up and holding on to her just in case the earth wanted to sallow her up again, and he was not going to let that happen. As all four guardians start to see what damage had been done to the throne room the whole castle started to shake and they felt the barrier come down. They looked around at each other wondering what had just happened. The doors to the throne flew opened and walked in all the maids and the Queen. Andrew walked over to his grandmother and hugged her so hard he took the breath out of her.

"Well done my grandson, and well-done guardians." Queen Ruth said.

"Thank you, grandmother, thank you your highness." Andrew and guardians said together.

"Andrew this is the girl you were telling me about and the reason you called off the wedding to Marilyn?" Queen Ruth asked.

"I'm sorry, but I could not marry someone I was not in love with. She also has another person she cares about very much. Please understand." Andrew said.

"I do my child, I'm glad that she is very strong, but she is young still. So, the marriage can wait." Queen said.

"Thank you so much grandmother." Andrew said running back to Sue and lifting her up.

"Now that we have took care of that, and Marcus is gone for good. Andrew, you have a choice to make." Queen Ruth said.

As Andrew looked puzzled, then thought about what was just said he knew what the Queen met. He smiled at his mother because he knew that he had a higher calling. He is the guardian of the Earth Realm and the Crown Prince who is in love with Sue.

"I choose to go as a guardian to look for the Star Princess and be with Sue." Andrew said.

"Well-chosen my child. Then guardian of light and travel you must explain things to him as well." Queen Ruth told Sue.

As Sue looked at Andrew, she started to cry and it was hard to find the words to tell him that he must return to the Crystal Star of Water and Ice with Faizah that he could not go with Joey and her on their mission to find the other guardians, because she only has enough power to take three at a time.

"What does she mean Sue?" Andrew asked.

"She means that you can't go with us to find the other guardians and that Faizah, and you have to return to the Crystal Star of Water and Ice." Joey said stepping up.

"WHAT!" Both Faizah and Andrew said together.

"What he means is that I don't have enough power to take all four of us to another realm." Sue said crying.

"You are telling me that after all this time I finally get to see you again just to say goodbye!" Andrew said with anger.

"Please don't say it like that we will be able to see each other again and I won't be alone Joey will be with me because this is our mission that we have to do. You have a different mission from us." Sue said.

"Putting it that way does not ease my mind on you going off by yourself." Andrew said.

"I understand what you mean, but we all do have a mission to do, and this happens to be ours. I will take good care of her, like I have been doing this whole time." Joey said.

"I understand, please be careful you two." Faizah said.

"Thanks Faizah, could you do me a favor when you two reach the Crystal Star of Water and Ice." Joey asked her.

"Yeah, what do you need?" Faizah asked.

"Please tell the other guardians we are fine and continuing our search for the other guardians. Let Lola know that I think of her every day we are part from each and that I'm looking forward to that day we are all together again." Joey said.

"Got it." Faizah said.

"Well guardian of light and travel there is a portal room right behind the curtains over there behind the throne chair please let us all go in there. That way you can open the portal to the Crystal Star of Water and Ice for these two." Ruth said.

"Okay." Sue said.

As everyone walked into the room hidden behind the curtain in the throne room, they see all kinds of mirrors and the one that was calling to her was off to the left. As she approached the mirror she reached out and touched it and the portal opened to the Crystal Star of Water and Ice. Sue knew this because she seen the school that her friends and her attended but is out for the summer.

"How will we know the guardians?" Faizah asked.

"They will sense you coming." Sue said.

"Okay." Faizah said.

Faizah was the first to enter the portal and then it was Andrew's turn, but before he goes through the portal he walks over to Sue and pulls her in, and kisses her on the lips, and it lasted a long minute before he stopped. He looked down at her, and tears fell from his eyes, and he kissed her again not caring who was watching them. Then he let her go and walked into the portal leaving Sue breathless.

****To Be Continued****

Coming to a bookstore near you. More adventures with the guardians in Land of the Crystal Stars: Last Rise of the Guardians.

Printed in the United States
by Baker & Taylor Publisher Services